Castell's Passion

Arabella Sheen

Copyright © 2022 Arabella Sheen
Published by priceplacebooks

A night in his arms, but it comes at a price. Will her heart survive?

Billionaire Marc Castell, owner of the Castell Hotel Group, isn't looking for love. His jet-set lifestyle means he's a 'love them and leave them' type of guy…that is, until **Kate McKenna** walks into his life.

Kate is on the warpath. Her underage sister is planning to spend a weekend in Paris with Marc's nephew, and she's determined to put a stop to the affair before it begins.

Marc has a plan of his own. He promises to save Kate's sister from his nephew, but there's a condition attached. Kate has to travel to Cannes with him and play the part of his girlfriend—including spending the night in his bed. But whenever Marc takes Kate in his arms his world is turned upside down, and he discovers he wants more from her than a casual weekend fling.

Kate has no time for sexy, powerful playboys. She's too busy building her career and expanding her catering business. But when she gets to know the man behind the façade, she wonders if she can resist the sensual attraction growing between them. Will she be seduced by his charm and sacrifice everything she believes in for one night of passion in his arms?

Marc has a battle on his hands as he strives to win Kate's love…and her heart.

CHAPTER ONE

"Mr. Castell, there's a Ms. Kate McKenna to see you, sir."

The door to Castell's office was ajar, and from across the spacious foyer, Kate could hear the receptionist asking him if he would see an unexpected visitor.

Kate heard his firm response. It was a loud, clear, and decisive "*No*."

Before Kate had time for second thoughts, she sprung from her chair, grabbed her handbag, and made a beeline across the hall toward the lion's den. She was like a torpedo on a self-destruct mission. Nothing was stopping her. Not even the defenseless receptionist guarding the door to the inner sanctum of Castell's office.

Barging into the room, Kate stood her ground. At last she was facing Castell—the man she'd come to see—and she wasn't moving...at least not until she'd said what she'd come to say.

The enemy was before her, and with an impatient, defiant toss of her head she waited undaunted for his reaction. None came. There was no backlash of anger and no verbal assault of harsh, insensitive words. The man remained silent.

A stony quietness filled the room, and without commentary, he observed her as if making a cold, calculating assessment of her. Sitting at his desk, he leaned backward, relaxing into the backrest of his swivel chair, and with dark, mysterious eyes he examined Kate from the top of her head to her feet, and he wasn't missing a thing.

Kate was dressed in a pair of faded jeans that was a size too small, and a skimpy cotton top which was a little too short. Some people might think her outfit looked casual and too sexy for such opulent surroundings, but today she didn't care what she looked like. She was in no mood to worry one iota what others thought.

She wasn't there to impress. She was there, at Castell House in Grosvenor Square, the headquarters of the Castell Hotel Group in London, to deliver her message and get her point across. She was going to make it crystal clear to Mr. "*Casanova*" Castell that he was to keep his hands off her sister Nikki.

Adrenaline was pumping through her veins, and she was ready to do battle. Even though her heart was hammering fiercely in her chest, she was holding her nerve.

She guessed Castell must be in his early thirties. Power and authority was oozing from him, and against her will, she found herself physically drawn toward him. There was an instant attraction, a compelling pull. And she didn't know if her anger was fueling her emotions or if it was his magnetism.

Now she understood why Nikki was attracted to him. She could see and feel the chemistry he radiated for herself. Castell was an impressive figure of a man and one look from those dark, piercing eyes left her enthralled.

Jet-black hair touched the collar of his crisp, white shirt. He was clean-shaven, bronzed, and an uber-smart dresser. At a guess she'd say he was wearing a hand-made Savile Row suit, but she could be wrong. His suit jacket was draped around the back of his chair, but it didn't really matter, because she knew that whatever Castell wore he would look like the high-powered finance magnet he was.

Standing in front of his desk, she was aware of his penetrating gaze. There was no mistaking the attraction in his eyes. He was assessing her, weighing her up, and Kate could tell by the slow, seductive smile showing on Castell's face that he was interested.

It had taken a lot of effort and nerve on her part to get past the barrage of security personnel protecting him. But she'd done it. And she was sure that was something very few people had managed to achieve.

In the stillness of the room Kate felt something stir deep within her, and for a brief moment she thought she saw a flicker of the same desire mirrored on his face.

Castell was the most magnificent looking man she'd ever seen, and as he shuffled the papers he'd been reading, she wondered what it would be like to feel those strong, masculine hands on her body. She could only imagine the heated torture they would inflict, but it was a heated torture she was certain any woman would be willing to endure.

He was sex on legs, and with his potent looks she could understand why, and how, any woman, including her sister, would feel sexually drawn to him. She sensed it would be so easy to succumb to his wishes and bend to his will.

"That will be all, Clair," Castell said to the receptionist in his deeply emphasized French accent.

Tingles ran up and down Kate's spine at the sound of his voice. That sexy voice was enough to make any woman go weak at the knees.

Clair left the room, and as the door closed behind her Castell pointed to a sofa at the far end of the room, indicating for Kate to sit down.

"Take a seat. I shan't be long," he said. Then, ignoring her as if she were no longer present in the room, he returned to the pile of paperwork in front of him.

Looking at the man working behind the desk, Kate realized he wasn't at all what she'd expected. She'd thought Eduardo Castell would be nearer Nikki's age. This man wasn't, and it made the situation worse than she'd originally thought it was. Castell was no young adolescent. He was a mature adult who was, at a guess, at least twice her sister's age.

"I need to talk to you about Nikki," she said with resolution in her voice. She wasn't going to be brushed off or dismissed out of hand. She was going to make herself heard.

"And I said sit." He didn't even look up.

Kate opened her mouth to protest, but then thought better of it. On trembling legs she went to the far side of the room, tossed her handbag carelessly onto one of the sofas, and taking a seat, waited for the overbearing, obnoxious Mr. Castell to finish what he was doing.

Kate couldn't relax. She was too on edge to sit still. Restless, she stood and wandered over to the high Georgian windows to look out at the elegant town houses in Grosvenor Square.

Most of the buildings were tall, resplendent structures, and Castell House was no exception. In fact, Castell House was one of the most elegant, imposing town addresses she'd ever been to. On the front façade of the house were two magnificent columns. There was also a lintel doorway and a porch entrance under which sat two imposing stone lions. When she first arrived at the Square she'd known it was a grand address in Central London, but she hadn't realized exactly how chic and impressive Castell House would be.

Looking across the road to the Square's splendid gardens, she noticed some mothers playing with their children near the fountain. Young lovers lay stretched out on blankets on the well-kept lawns, basking in the heat of the glorious afternoon. Seeing that, Kate wished she was anywhere but here. She didn't want to witness the pleasures and enjoyments of others when she was in such a horrible mood.

As the London traffic of cars and buses drove by, a flitting thought passed through her head that she ought to be spending her precious time in a better way. She should be working, not running around after Nikki's amorous admirer.

It had taken Kate several years of hard work to build up her catering business, and she was doing well. She was a successful business woman, and she was achieving what she'd set out to do. Her business was flourishing, and she was slowly but surely gaining a reputation as being one of the best events caterers in the business.

McKenna Catering had several on-going contracts with a select group of clients. The majority of her clientele were the rich elite of London, and they were willing to spend substantial amounts of money for the services she provided.

There were always parties and bookings to organize, and although Kate had an excellent team of workers covering events, she liked to be on hand to make sure things ran smoothly. Her clients were also keen to see her at their parties. Even if she only made a brief appearance before disappearing, they liked to know she was in charge and holding the reins.

Gazing out of the office windows there was time enough for Kate to surreptitiously study the man sitting at the desk. Castell was concentrating on the work in front of him, and she assumed he was unaware of her scrutiny from beneath her lashes. Looking him over, Kate couldn't find fault with his appearance.

He was incredibly gorgeous. The sharp, chiseled lines of his face and the thick mass of black hair were things she found attractive in a man. His body looked lean, strong, and powerful, and with his bronzed, sun-kissed skin and his dark looks, he looked almost princely.

When he moved to turn the pages of a document, or he reached for a file, the silky material of his shirt stretched, rippling across his wide shoulders, accentuating the muscles in his arms. Even though he was seated she could tell he was more than six-foot tall.

This man wasn't just a pen-pusher. He was fit, and it showed. He was also very sexy. There was no denying his magnetism, and although her sister might be a young, vulnerable teenager who had fallen head-over-heels for those dark, sensual eyes, Kate wasn't.

At twenty-four, Kate wasn't such an easy target when it came to men. Even though she'd never met this man before, she knew his type. She could spot a womanizer and playboy a mile off, and she avoided them like the plague.

She wanted nothing to do with men who used people, especially women, for their own pleasure. These men always discarded their lovers because they were no longer the flavor of the moment. Shallow, temporary relationships were something Kate had no time for, and with this type of man emotional investment was generally absent. Kate suspected she was looking at trouble, and it was trouble spelled with a capital "T".

As Castell reached up to loosen the knot of his tie he turned his head in Kate's direction. His piercing eyes locked onto hers. He held her spellbound and Kate's stomach flipped, sending her heart pulsating with unexpected excitement.

There was no protection from his penetrating gaze. He was looking her up and down, and it was as if his eyes were stripping her naked. Exposing her, and revealing all for his satisfaction and pleasure. And there was nothing she could do about it.

Castell was obviously enjoying the fact that the t-shirt she was wearing was too short. She'd been planning to take the morning off to catch up on some chores at home. Things that she never seemed to have time for. These days taking time off from her business was almost impossible. But then Nikki and her problems had intervened with her plans, and now she was here…in Castell's plush, stylish office dressed totally inappropriately in a t-shirt and jeans.

The short, skimpy t-shirt she was wearing left her feeling vulnerable and exposed. Although it covered her body, it didn't conceal her curves. And no matter how hard she pulled or tugged on the shirt it couldn't cover the small amount of exposed midriff that was showing. But that wasn't the worst of her problems. Gradually, Kate became aware that her nipples were beginning to show.

Compared to the warm heat of the spring sunshine outside, Castell's office was a cool haven from the balminess. The air conditioning was on full blast, and although it was cooling her overheated skin, that wasn't all it was cooling.

Kate wasn't wearing a bra, and as the cool air wafted gently over her body she discovered her nipples were hardening. The fabric of her top made the hard peaks obvious. Crossing her arms over her breasts, she hoped to conceal what was becoming visible, but it was to no avail. It didn't help. Castell had a clear view, and he was examining every detail of her body.

"How is a man supposed to concentrate with you staring at him?" he asked while running a hand through his hair in frustration.

Shrugging her shoulders, Kate remained silent. She didn't care if he couldn't concentrate. And she hadn't been staring at him. Or had she? At least, she didn't think she had.

"Mr. Castell..." She uncrossed her arms and straightened to her full height of five feet, four inches.

"Yes...Ms. McKenna." He sat back and threw down the pen he'd been holding, giving Kate his full attention.

"We have to talk."

"So you told me. If I remember correctly, it has something to do with someone by the name of Nikki."

"Of course it's about Nikki. Who else would it be about?" Kate snapped.

He looked startled at her heated outburst, but he waited silently for her to continue.

Kate was a confident woman with plenty of self-assurance, but in this instance she sensed she was out of her depth. She knew she had a fight on her hands. There was a battle to win, and even though her confidence was ebbing she knew she had to stay strong. She had to fight this arrogant man and bring

Nikki back from the brink of a disastrous affair with Eduardo Castell.

Although the Castells had amassed a huge amount of real estate and wealth over the years, it was still classed as *new money*. Kate knew of the Castells—anyone who read glossy magazines or daily newspapers knew who they were. They were a global name. Royalty of the hotel world. And surprisingly, Nikki was working for them as part of her school work experience.

The Castells were the elite. The *crème de la crème*. Out of reach. And with Nikki starting at the bottom, supposedly learning the ropes, Kate hadn't expected her sister to actually come into contact with any of them.

It was now beginning to look like the work experience, which was meant to be such a positive and educational encounter, was backfiring. Kate's worst fear was that Castell was abusing his authority and using his privileged position to influence Nikki into acting inappropriately. She thought he'd persuaded Nikki into having an affair, and nothing and no one was going to prevent her from stopping this man taking advantage of Nikki. She was on the war path.

Still standing beside the window Kate thrust her trembling hands behind her back, hiding them from view. She didn't want to reveal how nervous she was, but her action was a big mistake, because it only accentuated her breasts even more.

"You do understand that I can't let Nikki go with you, don't you?" she asked.

The man looked ruthless. She thought reasoning with him was her best option. She was certain she wasn't going to become emotional or fly into a temper, which she tended to do when championing a cause, but she knew anything was possible; and anything could happen. The situation was volatile.

"You must see how impossible this is," she said, searching his face for a reaction. "You can't take a young teenager away with you, even if she does work for you."

Kate had *inherited* her teenage sister when their parents died in a car crash, and until a short while ago things had been going well between them. They had a good sisterly relationship. As the older sister, Kate had always looked after Nikki, and although there was almost a seven-year age gap between them, they were close and shared their adventures with each other. That was...until now.

It was only after Nikki went to work at The Castell Hotel on schoolwork experience that things started to take a turn for the worse. Her sister had gone into rebellion mode, and Nikki's unexpected defiance was causing Kate concern.

When she'd learned of Nikki's plans, she'd gone straight to The Castell Hotel with the intention of confronting Eduardo. She was going to call a halt to the romance that was blossoming between Eduardo Castell and Nikki, but Castell wasn't at the hotel.

Having spoken to hotel reception, telling them that she'd like to see Mr. Castell, the reply from a very curvy receptionist at the front desk had been a mumbled, suggestive, "Who wouldn't?" And with those words ringing in her ear, Kate was left in no doubt that Castell was a heartthrob and a heartbreaker extraordinaire.

"So...Nikki's a teenager, is she?" he asked.

"Yes, she is, and I'm still her legal guardian until she turns eighteen, which won't happen for several months. If you take her to Cannes, you do realize I'll have to report you to the authorities, don't you?"

"Me? Take a woman to Cannes? Now there's an idea."

"Yes. Your secretary said that's where you're headed."

"Ah, yes. Of course...Cannes and the Anistons."

"Nikki said she was going away with you. I hadn't realized you intended to take her out of the country."

Standing up from his desk, he walked toward her like a panther zoning in on his prey. He came to a stop in front of her. The man towered above her, and she had to tilt her head back to look up at him.

He was close. Dangerously close. They were face-to-face, and sparks were flying. She could feel the palpable tension pulsating between them.

"Ms. McKenna...Kate. It wounds me to think you believe I'm capable of having an affair with a teenager. Let me put your mind at rest. It's not my intention to take Nikki out of the country...especially now that I've seen you."

"You mean you're not taking Nikki to Cannes?"

"No, but I'm quite willing to take you along for the ride instead. That is...if you'd like to accompany me," he said, arching an eyebrow in a suggestive manner.

Kate took in the full meaning behind his evocative words and was shocked beyond belief. How dare he proposition her in that way. Surely he was joking? And did he think she was the type of woman who would do that? The audacity of the man!

CHAPTER TWO

Marc Castell had known many women. He was the head of the large family firm, and was in the billion-dollar bracket of *successful*. As an eligible bachelor he was much sought after, and some women connived, cajoled, or bribed their way into his social circle in order to meet him. Their aim was always the same. They all wanted to get to know Marc on an intimate level, hoping for a lasting relationship. But Marc wasn't into long-term commitment. When it came to women and matters of the heart he was a 'love them and leave them' type of guy. Over the years he'd become cynical. He'd had to harden his heart against the women of the world, and he'd grown cold to their needs, and uncaring to the point of callousness.

Inheriting the Castell fortune at an early age Marc soon learned what the women in his life wanted from him. It was one thing and one thing only—his money.

He knew it was the erotic pull of his wealth that was the main attraction. He'd had lots of affairs and been approached or propositioned in many ways before, but so far none of the women had used their sister as an excuse to get close. He found it fascinating, even intriguing, and he wondered what Kate's next move would be.

Kate had a sensuality that was breathtakingly beautiful. The soft curves of her body and the full roundness of her breasts had him wanting to reach out and touch her. But that wasn't all. There was also an elusive quality that made him want to possess her. As a connoisseur of fine art he knew perfection when he saw it, and as a collector of fine things...he wanted.

When Kate had mentioned Cannes she had reminded him of where he had to be this weekend. It was somewhere he didn't particularly want to be, but there was no avoiding his responsibilities. This weekend he was spending time with the Anistons, and although they were good friends, this wasn't a social occasion. This was business.

Marc was in the middle of negotiating a hotel-travel deal, and there was to be an informal party to which the Aniston's board of directors had also been summoned. They needed to discuss some of the finer details of the proposed contract, and negotiations were going to be tricky.

With Kate's unexpected suggestion, Marc decided he could use a woman at his side while he was in Cannes. And he wanted this woman.

"How dare you?" Kate said, as if she was infuriated he would even suggest that she go to Cannes with him.

It was obvious Kate had great difficulty controlling her temper, and he wondered if she was about to lash out and strike. She didn't.

"Oh, I dare," he said, and he took a step nearer.

He was now so close to her that he was able to run an exploring finger along her soft cheek and then down her slender neck until he reached the hollow at its base. Surprisingly, she didn't flinch away, and by the hot flush on her cheeks he could tell that his touch was having the desired effect. He was burning her with caresses. Her skin was warm, and as he continued to stroke he felt her tremble in anticipation.

Kate took a step back, but he followed, taking two steps forward so that their bodies were lightly connecting. He could feel her erect nipples pressing against the material of his shirt, and he had to stifle a groan.

Kate's breathing quickened, and he saw desire flash briefly in her eyes before it was replaced with anger. He wrapped his arms around her and pressed their bodies even closer together. She struggled, pushing against his shoulders, but her struggles were half-hearted at best.

Capturing her hands, he moved them behind her back, holding them imprisoned. Then Marc heard a soft moan of longing escape her lips. The fight had left her, and as she rested her head against his chest he knew she was silently conceding defeat. He had won.

Cradling her in his arms, slowly, ever so slowly, he lowered his lips down to meet and caressingly touch hers. Her lips were soft and pliant, and as he held her helpless against his onslaught her mouth parted, forming an anguished, "*No.*"

"*No* what?" he asked, whispering the words as he nuzzled against the delicate shell-like lobe of her ear.

With one hand still holding hers behind her back, his other hand began gently caressing the line of her jaw. Moving to her mouth, he parted her lips with his thumb, and with a light, delicate touch he explored. Kate gave a strangled whimper.

"There will never be a *no* between us, Kate," he said softly, his words a promise. "There will only ever be *yes*." He smiled slightly as his gaze searched her face, and then he saw the desperate longing shining in her eyes.

"You can't...I won't let you," she murmured as she trembled against him.

But her protests were futile. He wasn't taking no for an answer. Touching her full, moist lips with his, he began a raw, bruising invasion of her senses. His kisses were intentionally rough as he searched for a response from deep within her...and he found it.

Kate's protests were silenced as he plundered her mouth, taking the kisses he wanted, and she surrendered to him.

Marc released his grip on her hands, and with her hands now free, Kate clutched at the material of his shirt. Marc locked his hands around her bared, slender waist, and with long, slow, drawn-out movements he moved upward, cupping the soft mounds of her breasts over her shirt. He heard a sharp intake of breath, and he knew it to be a gasp of pleasurable delight. He was turning her on, and it was giving him a sense of power.

From the first moment they had laid eyes on each other there had been an instant attraction, a sort of electric chemistry between them. And he suspected he was affecting Kate as much as she was affecting him.

Marc Castell—the cold, calculating, playboy billionaire with a heart of steel—was melting. He craved Kate with an urgent need, and he knew by her reaction the feeling was mutual.

"What is it you want from me?" she asked as she tried to break free. Her protests were ineffectual.

"I think you know what I want," he said. "*I want you*. I want everything you have to offer." He knew his words were brutal; they had to be, because he was serious.

"I'm not available, and I have nothing to offer you."

"Well...we'll have to try and change that, won't we?" he said, and he wasn't joking.

Kate blinked as if she was trying to wake from a dream, and then from somewhere in the room the sound of a cellphone's ringtone broke the silence.

The continual ringing was claiming Marc's attention, and with great reluctance he released Kate from his embrace, but not before he had given her another long, possessive kiss.

"Stay where you are," he commanded, and then running his hands through his hair in frustration, he walked over to his desk.

Picking up the cellphone, he flicked open the case.

"Castell here," he said. Then looking directly at Kate he continued to talk. "Yes, this is Marc Castell speaking."

Marc heard Kate's shocked gasp as the penny drop. She was processing the fact that she'd been talking to the wrong man and that he wasn't Nikki's boyfriend, Eduardo. Kate had finally discovered he was *Marc* Castell.

* * * *

Marc continued talking on the cellphone, and by the way he paced back and forth across the room it was obvious something was worrying him.

"Thanks, Hal. Good work. Have the jet fueled and on stand-by. I'll let you know what we're doing on this end. As far as I'm concerned, I'm still scheduled to fly to Cannes this afternoon, but who knows? I'll get back to you when I know what's happening."

After a short pause Marc clicked off the cellphone and turned to Kate.

"Which do you want first? The good news or the bad?" he asked, and it was done in such a manner that it sent shivers of dread down Kate's spine.

His chiseled features were hard, like granite, and there was a visible pulse throbbing along the angle of his sharp jawline. Something was wrong.

"You're not Eduardo?"

"No...not Eduardo."

"But your secretary said..."

"Clair showed you in here and you assumed I was Eduardo. As I've already told you, I'm not him. He's my nephew."

"Ohhh..." Kate was at a loss for words.

"That's the good news," he stated bluntly.

Marc didn't return to his office chair. Instead, he walked around to the front of his solid, oak desk, leaned back against it, and with his arms folded across his chest, he waited.

"And the bad news?" she asked, wanting to know the worst.

"That was my pilot on the phone. He thought he saw Eduardo at the airport...with a girl. Hal's made enquiries and he's found out Eduardo's booked two seats on a commercial flight to Paris. Knowing how I'd react, Hal phoned to tell me. You see, Eduardo's had previous entanglements with women and he's not always come off unscathed. Until now I've had no reason to intervene or meddle, but there was one woman who—"

"I don't believe what I'm hearing. What do you mean his entanglements with women? Actually, don't bother answering that. I think I get the picture," she told him with a disgruntled tone. "You've told me all I need to know about Eduardo, and all I can say is—it must run in the family. Like nephew, like uncle. The Castell womanizers."

Now more than ever, Kate was determined that Nikki was to have nothing to do with the Castell dynasty.

"It sounds worse than it is," he said, dismissing her concerns as he shrugged his shoulders. "Boys will be boys, and men will be men."

"What makes you think it's Nikki who's with Eduardo? It might not be her."

Kate was hopeful, but she suspected that when she'd left the house that morning her worst fears had come true. More than likely Nikki had disobeyed instructions to stay at home and had rushed to be with Eduardo.

"I didn't say the woman with Eduardo was Nikki, but do you want to take that chance, or do you want to follow me to the airport and find out for sure?"

"I'm going call Nikki first," she told him.

"Go ahead," he said with indifference and passed his cellphone over for Kate to use. "I hope you realize we're wasting precious time. And while you're phoning, more than likely they'll be boarding and taking off." Digging his hands deep into his trouser pockets, Marc waited while Kate dialed Nikki's number.

When Kate got no response and realized Nikki wasn't going to answer her cellphone or pick up the house phone, she looked across at Marc as if it was his fault. Passing his cellphone back to him, she had to admit defeat.

* * * *

Marc didn't need Kate to tell him that Nikki wasn't reachable. He could tell by the defeated look on Kate's face. It seemed he was right after all. Nikki was with Eduardo...and they were gone.

Marc supposed it would now fall on his shoulders to track them down, but if he was honest with himself he didn't want to become entangled in something that was none of his business. He had his own affairs to take care of this weekend. He had places to be, people to see, and things to do. He didn't have time to babysit two young people who had disappeared somewhere for a clandestine destination and were off playing *lovebirds*.

"You have to stop him. Tell Eduardo to bring Nikki home," she demanded.

So, Kate was expecting him to instantly solve the problem of the disappearing couple. But he wasn't being backed into a corner, and he wasn't being told what to do.

"Why should I do that? I'm not Eduardo's keeper. He's old enough to make his own decisions."

"Eduardo might be old enough to decide what he wants to do, but in many ways Nikki is still a baby. All right, I admit that since the loss of our parents I might be overly protective of her, but it's so hard to let go of someone you care for. Even though I know at some point I will have to let her move on, I can't. Not just yet. My sister's too young to experience the disappointments of adulthood, and she's never had any real, true experience with men," she told him anxiously.

"I thought you said she's almost eighteen."

"But that doesn't make her an adult. Just because she looks like a woman doesn't make her a woman. You men don't understand, or you don't want to understand." Kate let out a frustrated sound of anger. "All men are the same. You're only out for one thing. And if Eduardo should harm her in any way, I'm warning you now...I'll make him pay for it."

"And how will you do that?" Marc asked with disdain, but Kate ignored his cynical question, dismissing it out of hand.

"It's obvious you're not going to be of any help to me," she said, sounding vexed.

"What exactly is it you expect me to do?" he asked.

What happened between Eduardo and Nikki was of no interest to Marc. He didn't care one way or another if the young couple had flown to France for a brief affair or not. His only concern was that the Castell fortune, and in this particular instance Eduardo's fortune, remained intact.

"I expect you to stop him. Tell him to leave Nikki alone," was Kate's frank reply.

Marc shrugged and raised his hands as if powerless to do anything. It was a typical French gesture.

He was reluctant to listen to Kate's problems. He simply didn't want to get involved. Being gallant and helping a stunning, beautiful woman was one thing, but taking on the problems of that woman's sister was altogether another ball game.

"I can't. Or rather I won't try and stop him," he said with brutal honesty.

Marc had no desire to curb Eduardo's extracurricular activities, but if he had to, he was willing to put a stop to Nikki's exploits. He had no idea what her motive was in striking up a friendship with Eduardo, but from his own experience women generally got involved with a Castell for one reason and one reason only—money.

"You have to stop them," Kate insisted anxiously. "If Nikki and Eduardo leave the country, they will soon be out of reach, and it will be beyond my power to stop the inevitable from happening. You have to do something."

"I don't have to do anything." His reply was candid and to the point.

"Talking to you is like banging my head against a brick wall. It's obvious you're a stubborn man. Why won't you do something?"

Marc always kept his involvement with Eduardo to a strict minimum. Only once, when a gold digger got her claws into his nephew, bleeding him dry of his money and threatening to accept Eduardo's proposal of marriage, did Marc step in and call a halt to the affair.

Usually he never interfered, so he didn't know why he was considering doing just that. But thinking about it he decided that perhaps it was because of the way Kate's beseeching, dusky eyes were looking at him. Seeing Kate's distress made him want to help.

He had a sudden undeniable urge to protect her from anything that could cause anguish. He wanted to shield her, safeguard her, and save her from any hurt that might come her way.

"If you won't do anything to help, I'll have to go to the airport and find her myself." Kate waited, expecting a response.

When Marc saw her genuine concern and apprehension for her sister he knew he couldn't stand on the sideline any longer. He decided he would have to step in and take action.

"All right," he said. "Let's suppose I'm prepared to do what you ask—what are you willing to do for me in return? What would you sacrifice to get your sister back?"

There was a long silence as Kate digested what he'd said. She then looked at him as if wondering if she'd heard correctly.

"Why are we wasting time talking about what I would sacrifice? Surely it would be best if we both went to the airport and stopped the two runaways from leaving the country before it's too late."

"I'm still waiting for your answer. What are you prepared to forfeit to guarantee the safety of your sister?" Marc asked again.

"Anything," she said innocently. "I'll do anything. What is it you need me to do?"

"You promise to do *anything*? Are you sure you mean that?"

Marc wanted to make absolutely certain everything was clear between them. He needed to know Kate was willing to do whatever was necessary to get her sister back.

"Of course I'm sure. I would do anything for Nikki. She's my sister." There was a deep conviction in Kate's voice as she said those words.

"Good. I'll remind you of this conversation in a few hours' time, but for now we'd better get moving." Marc began clearing his desk of some papers and packing his briefcase. "We'll stop off at your place to collect your passport. Where do you live?"

"Why do I need my passport?" she asked, puzzled. "Won't we be able to stop them at the airport?"

"You'll need your passport because if my guess is correct, they're already on board the plane and on their way to Paris."

"Ohhh..."

"If we're going after them—"

"No *if*s," Kate interrupted. "I'm following them even if you're not. I have to go. You can stay here if you like. In fact, I'd prefer it if you stayed. I can manage on my own."

Marc suspected Kate would be out of her depth when it came to reining in the two weekend elopers. He thought it best if he stepped in and tackled the situation, as he suspected his voice would carry more weight and effectiveness should there be problems.

He also thought it would be a good opportunity, during the flight, to get to know Kate a little better before presenting her with his proposal. And according to their agreement, and having promised she would do anything he asked, he knew it was a proposal she had no option but to accept. Little did Kate know what Marc had in store for her!

"You're coming with me to Paris," he told her, and his tone implied there would be no discussion on the subject.

"But I don't want to go with you," she persisted. Her protests fell on deaf ears.

"No buts. That's the end of it. Now tell me where you live."

He wasn't going to back down. He was in business mode, and with an insistent look of determination in his eyes, Kate reluctantly conceded. She gave in.

"Our house is on the other side of London," she warned as she went over to the sofa to collect the handbag she'd discarded earlier. "We're in Eltham, which is south of the river. I'll phone Patty, my assistant, and ask her to collect my passport and bring it to the airport. Which one are we flying from?"

"Heathrow. But it will be quicker if we drive over to your place. You can pack an overnight bag at the same time. Anything you forget we can always buy in Paris."

Without ceremony he began ushering Kate out of the office, steering the way over toward reception.

"Would you have the car brought around, please, Clair? And would you phone the Anistons in Cannes? Tell them I'm delayed. Say I'll be joining them sometime this weekend and that I'll be there as soon as I can get away. You can also warn them I'm bringing someone with me."

"Yes, sir. Anything else?"

Marc looked pointedly in Kate's direction as he spoke.

"For some unknown reason the document I was working on hasn't been completed. It's on my desk with the other papers. If you could lock them away in the safe that would be great, and I'll sign them when I get back. You can also tell Cade to cancel the Italian meeting. Put the deal on hold."

"Yes, sir." Clair looked at Marc as if amazed that he was leaving the building without having signed the takeover contract.

Marc was a little surprised by it himself. Cade Knightley, the company's accountant and a good friend of Marc's, was waiting for the all clear on the

Italian takeover bid before going ahead with the deal. Time was of the essence. But it seemed this afternoon Marc had other pressing priorities to take care of.

While Marc was busy issuing instructions to Clair, he could see Kate was impatient to be on their way.

"Miss McKenna and I will be upstairs in my apartment. You can buzz me when the car arrives, and we'll come down. Oh, and should anyone wish to contact us, we'll be staying in Paris tonight."

"Together?" asked Clair discreetly.

"Yes," Marc said with conviction. "We'll be together." And there was no mistaking his hidden meaning.

CHAPTER THREE

The doors to the lift closed, confining Marc and Kate in the restricted space. Reaching for the control panel, he set the lift in motion, whisking them silently upward.

Once again Marc was only inches away from Kate, and as her body brushed for a fleeting moment against his, a burst of soft, scented perfume filled his nostrils. His senses were stirred. In the confines of the lift, and with the air charged with their body heat, they could almost smell the sexual tension between them.

"We should have taken the stairs," he said, and she nodded in agreement.

"Why do I need an overnight case?" Kate asked, breaking the silence.

"You might not need one. There's a possibility that we don't have to stay overnight. It depends what Eduardo has planned," he explained. "My guess is that by the time we get to Paris it will be evening, and it might not be worth the bother of arranging a flight for tonight. Remember, we still have to find them. Once I know where their flight has landed I can put a trace on them, and if it goes well it shouldn't be too difficult to track them down."

"It's kind of you to do this," she said politely. "It's not as if you know Nikki personally. Or do you? Although she works for you, you haven't actually met her, have you?"

"No, I haven't."

"Then why are you concerned about her? Do you know more than you're telling me? Perhaps you know something about Nikki and Eduardo I don't."

"Let's get this clear. I'm not concerned for Nikki. I'm doing this for Eduardo."

"Ohhh..." She looked a little confused by his words. "But surely Eduardo's a grown man and able to take care of himself. Why are you worried about him? Is it because I might still have him arrested?"

"No," he said with confidence. "The threat of an arrest doesn't bother me, because I doubt you will have grounds to make a charge or get a conviction. And even if someone were to make enquiries, I'd expect Eduardo to say he and Nikki were *just good friends* and were having a weekend away together. Normally I don't intervene in my nephew's affairs. I let him make his own mistakes, but on this occasion I'm being cautious. To be honest, my main concern is that you—the McKenna family—are after the Castell fortune. Who knows, perhaps you and your sister are scammers."

"Scammers?" asked Kate, horrified.

"Perhaps you're out to blackmail a Castell into marriage. It wouldn't be the first time a gold digger has been hoping to strike it rich by fleecing a Castell of his millions."

"Did you say blackmail?" she asked in disbelief.

"Why is that so hard to believe? I can assure you there have been many attempts, by many women, to get to our money. They all wanted marriage or some form of financial security."

"Well, you can keep your money and everything that goes with it," Kate said fiercely, losing control of her emotions. "I wouldn't have anything to do with you even if you were to pay me. Or is that it? Have I hit the nail on the head? Is that the way you get your women? You bribe them and pay for their services with money and gifts. Perhaps it's you who's the blackmailer. Do you use extortion and force them to give you their love in exchange for *payment*?"

At that moment the lift came to a smooth, noiseless halt, and as the doors slid open to reveal the apartment, Marc made a quick exit.

He had to get away, out of range of her scathing tongue. Once he was a safe distance from her, he turned to look back. But it wasn't Kate he was seeing…it was Agnés.

Marc didn't tell Kate that when he was a young, inexperienced man, feeling his way in the world, he'd become involved with an older woman. It was during his time as a student at one of France's elite *grande écoles*. He'd been nearing the end of his studies and had already sat most of his end exams, which were in business studies and tourism, when Agnés, one of the visiting lecturers, showed an interest in him.

Against all rules and regulations concerning lecturers and students fraternizing together, Agnés began to single him out for attention. Her interest in him began slowly. At first she questioned him during lectures, praising him and admiring his course work, and then gradually her fascination increased. Somehow she discovered which cafés he frequented with his friends, and she followed him, claiming it was coincidence or fate that they both happened to be drinking at the same place at the same time.

And then she had turned on her charm, and Marc had succumbed. He'd been captivated, beguiled, and had fallen completely under her spell. In his naiveté he'd thought Agnés had been attracted to *him*. He'd wanted to believe she was drawn to his alert mind and to his intelligence, but he'd been proven wrong.

One night, having arranged to meet Agnés for dinner, he'd entered the building where she lived and found the door to her apartment unlocked. Entering unannounced, and calling out her name, he walked through into the empty lounge. He could hear the sound of running water coming from the bathroom and assumed Agnés was in the shower getting ready for their night together.

Their evenings usually ended back at her place, and more often than not it wasn't until the sun was rising over the Parisian rooftops that Agnés allowed Marc to leave her bed and return to his rooms on campus. She was a demanding lover, and Marc in his innocence became besotted.

"Take a seat, Marc," she'd shouted to him through the bathroom door, and he had.

For a fleeting moment he wondered if he should join her beneath the hot spray, but then he heard the shower being turned off, followed by the noise of drawers and doors opening and closing, which indicated she was getting dressed.

Instead of sitting on the sofa or in one of the large easy armchairs Marc had taken a seat at her work desk. Her laptop was still on. The screen was on stand-by but she hadn't logged off.

Touching the keyboard, the screen sprang to life and what it revealed sent warning bells ringing in his head. On screen was a selection of web pages and it was obvious Agnés was researching his family and their hotel business. She was delving into his private life, and it was clear she had an abnormal interest in his financial success. But what annoyed him most was the fact she hadn't bothered to ask him about his background...she was researching.

When Agnés appeared from the bedroom and could see he'd discovered what she'd been doing, Marc had stood, faced her, and said, "Goodbye."

His message was loud and clear. Agnés knew there would be no reasoning with him. Marc had seen what there was to see and he'd made his decision then and there.

He'd discovered Agnés thought of him as her next meal ticket, and it had left a lasting impression. It was an impression that he'd never forgotten...nor forgiven.

In hindsight Marc was thankful for the lessons he'd learned from his encounter. He'd learned the hard way not to put his trust in beautiful women. But more importantly, his life had been shaped and changed forever by his first love affair. And that was the reason he now distrusted Kate and Nikki. He believed they too could be after the Castell billions.

* * * *

Standing in the middle of his apartment Kate noticed there was stony resentment showing in Marc's troubled eyes. He was holding onto his temper with tight control, and she realized her harsh words about him buying a woman's love had hit a sensitive spot. Maybe it was because there was some truth to them? Did he shower women with gifts, using it as a way to pay for their services, for the time he spent with them, and to buy their intimate friendship?

"One day you just might go too far and say something you shouldn't," he cautioned. "And if that were to happen, I'm warning you...you'll live to regret it."

As Marc walked away she was left shocked and stunned.

"I hope so," she called after him. She was speaking to him in a way she'd never dared speak before. "I hope I say something and it hits you where it hurts you the most."

Stopping in his tracks, he turned to face her and waited until she reached him.

"Save your anger and temper for someone else, Kate. It's wasted on me." His voice was deadly serious, and his eyes had a hard look of steel about them. "Listen to me, and listen carefully. I don't allow anyone to dictate to me or speak to me in that way, and you are no exception. Do we understand each other?"

His message came through loud and clear. There was no mistaking the meaning behind his words. She was being made to realize that Marc wouldn't tolerate such behavior and that there would be consequences if she were to do the same thing again.

"And let me tell you," she said daringly. "I don't take insults from anyone either. You've accused me of blackmail. Is it any wonder I want to get back at you?"

She was angry, and her temper was still flaring. When Marc said she could be plotting with her sister to blackmail the Castell family and that they were gold diggers, she found his harsh words provoking. As a result, she was reacting in a way that was totally out of character, she was lashing out at him.

Never before had she wanted to hurt someone in anger. But today she'd wanted to teach Marc a lesson. She meant to hurt this powerful man emotionally, in the same way he was hurting her.

She didn't know why she was behaving in such an unreasonable manner, but she was. Never before had she resorted to this type of reckless behavior, and now that she'd vented her wrath she felt she'd made a fool of herself. Kate didn't suffer fools easily, and she suspected neither did Marc. Both of them were perfectionists; not only in their work but also in their daily lives.

In search of perfection Kate was quite flexible in her outlook whereas Marc seemed rigid in his demands of excellence. And she decided that the two of them couldn't have been more similar in their personalities...yet so unalike in their work methods.

"Well..." she said. "I'm waiting for an apology."

"For what?" he asked.

"For calling me...for calling us—the McKennas—blackmailers."

"You have yet to prove otherwise," he said, and then he gave her a smile that was bordering on the edge of unpleasant.

Marc had made some horrid accusations against her, and she wasn't backing down until he'd said sorry. Still in a rage, she placed her hands on her hips, and standing in an aggressive stance, she was preparing to challenge him. But it was the wrong move to make. Her short, skimpy t-shirt was now pulled tightly across her breasts and her erect nipples were showing clearly through the material.

Kate could feel Marc's gaze being drawn toward her round, pert peaks. He was devouring her with his eyes, and his sexual hunger was becoming all the more evident for her to see. Uncontrollably, the sparks of rage she was feeling toward him began turning into flames of desire equal to his. They were both experiencing the same burning passion for one another.

"I shouldn't be long," he said. "I'm going to pack my flight bag and take a quick shower. Feel free to look around while you're waiting."

"Thanks," she said in an offhanded manner. She didn't know how he could master his feelings and cool off so quickly when that hot, burning desire was still deep inside her. Were all men like that? Able to turn hot and cold at will?

"Make yourself a coffee if you like. The kitchen's downstairs." Marc sauntered away into an adjacent room, and it was only after he disappeared from sight that she realized he still hadn't apologized for his blackmail accusations.

Although the man infuriated her, when she'd told him she would do anything for her sister, she hadn't been lying. Nikki was all the family she had left. And while she believed in allowing everyone to make their own mistakes, Nikki wasn't quite eighteen and she certainly wasn't old enough or wise enough to the ways of the world for a whirlwind romance—at least not yet. So, Kate was indeed prepared to do whatever it took to bring her sister home.

Pushing her thoughts aside, Kate looked around at her surroundings. From the moment she had walked through the front door of Castell House she hadn't known what to expect. She certainly hadn't anticipated the house would have an apartment above the office space, or that the apartment would be so large, or so grand.

The whole building was a big surprise. In the lift Marc had pressed the button for the sixth floor so she knew there was another floor above. The building was huge, gigantic, and the apartment appeared to be one massive rabbit warren of interconnecting rooms.

Wandering around the spacious sitting room, she found the décor impressive. It was decorated in a comfortable designer, shabby, chic style. A wide, chunky sofa and two armchairs were standing beside what looked to be a working fireplace. There was also a grand piano in the room. She'd noticed Marc had the long, slender fingers of a pianist and wondered if he played.

Marc came back out holding a packed flight bag and he set it beside the lift door, apparently leaving it there in readiness for collection when they left the apartment.

"Haven't you made coffee yet? Black, two sugars," he told her in a laidback, casual manner. "Or you can wait until I've showered and I'll make it."

It seemed his mood had changed. He'd gone from being the demanding aggressor to being an attentive host in a matter of seconds.

"Yes, sir...oh, *Master Sir*," she called out after him sarcastically.

What was he thinking? Did he think she didn't have a spine or that he could walk over her without a reaction? Well, he could think again. She wasn't there to do his bidding. He could find someone else to cater to his needs. She was sure there were plenty of women who would be willing to do it.

Marc came back and stood in the doorway. He looked serious.

"Kate...I'll be your master if that's what you'd like me to be, but as a general rule I prefer to be on equal footing with my woman."

"Your women...*your women*?" she asked, stunned. She couldn't believe he would dare say such a thing to her.

"You weren't listening," he told her. "I said *my woman*." And unexpectedly, he came over to where she was standing and lightly caressed her cheek. It was as if he'd had a sudden urge, almost a need, to connect emotionally and physically with her.

Turning away, Marc went back into the bedroom, leaving the door ajar. Kate stared after him opened-mouthed, gaping in amazement.

The man was impossible. One minute it seemed he was accusing her of blackmail and the next moment he was offering a relationship.

With the door to the bedroom open he was in plain view and it was as if something was compelling her to look. Her eyes were drawn to him as he moved about the bedroom, and with his back toward her she watched mesmerized as Marc began to strip off his clothes. From where she was standing she had an uninterrupted view of his dark, tanned, muscular torso.

When dressed Marc looked handsome and elegant, but naked he was much, much more. His broad, powerful body and long legs were clearly visible, and it was obvious he was all male.

He was a work of art. He was perfection. In other words...he was magnificent.

Looking at Marc was like indulging in a secret guilty pleasure, and Kate hastily turned away before he had a chance to notice she was gazing transfixed at his naked body.

"I'll make the coffee," she said to no one in particular, and disappearing below stairs she decided she could hide there, out of sight and out of reach of his shower antics. It would also be a place where she would feel safe from temptation.

It wasn't too long before Marc had finished showering and dressing, and he had come in search of her. Ten minutes ago dressed in a Savile Row suit he'd looked efficient and business-like, now, having showered and changed into a pair of stonewashed jeans along with a casual shirt, he looked ruggedly sexy. Not only did he dress down nicely, he also looked extremely relaxed, refreshed, and revitalized.

Marc took a sip of the strong, hot coffee she had poured for him.

"Not bad," he said while looking at her over the rim of the coffee cup. "In fact, it's quite good."

"You seem surprised."

"I am. Not everyone can make good coffee."

"But I'm a caterer. I ought to be able to make coffee."

"Being a caterer doesn't automatically give you the skills to make good coffee."

Marc practically downed the hot, aromatic liquid in one go before holding out his cup for more, and Kate thought that perhaps he might have a cast iron clad stomach.

"As it's so good, I think I'll let you pour me another," he said.

Kate set her own cup back onto its saucer and, without thinking, reached for the coffee pot. It was an automatic gesture, an inbred reflex. And although it was in her nature to be helpful she wasn't about to let him walk all over her. She wasn't going to allow any man to tell her what to do...was she? After all, she had a spine...didn't she?

"Are you always so demanding and bossy?" she asked, staring at him.

"Always."

"Then I pity anyone who has to live with you."

"Oh, I'm sure you could get used to it," he said, tongue in cheek. And there was a glimmer of humor shining in his eyes as he said those words.

Kate calmed the pounding of her heart. She had to think logically, not emotionally.

"No, I couldn't," she told him, arching a brow. "And I can't believe anyone would willingly want to get used to living with...*you*." But as she said those words she wasn't sure she was telling the truth. Apart from Marc being sexy and forceful, there was also something charming and charismatic about the man—even though he was arrogantly all male.

Marc Castell had a charisma any woman would fall for.

Despite what Kate had said she was certain she could get used to living with him, and living the luxurious life he had to offer. It had an appeal. But she knew she'd be out of her depth if she lived in his billionaire world. She would drown and lose her identity if she started a relationship with Marc. His lifestyle was fast-paced, extreme, and sometimes even dangerous. She wasn't sure she was willing to take on that sort of existence.

She feared that in order to fit into his world she would have to sacrifice her own ambitions, and that was something she wasn't prepared to do...for any man.

In the long run Kate knew they wouldn't be compatible.

She wanted to be her own woman. In fact, she needed to be her own woman and not someone Marc took along for the ride.

* * * *

Marc was a man of instant decisions. In his line of work he had to be. With the responsibility of running a billion-dollar hotel chain there was no room for error. He had to make the right choice, every time. He often made snap decisions based on facts presented to him, and in this case he'd already made his decision about Kate.

Without Kate having to throw out any lures she'd caught him. At first sight he'd fallen hook, line, and sinker for her. He was like a boy with a new toy, and he wanted to play with what he saw.

At all costs he was determined to get to know her better and to see where things went from there. He was also certain he wasn't letting her out of his sight until he got what he wanted, and he wanted...*Kate*.

"You might change your mind," he warned.

"Even if you paid me a million dollars I wouldn't want to live with you," she said, unyielding in her determination to resist him.

"Everyone has a price. How about two million?" he offered with a wink.

There wasn't time for her to react because at that moment the intercom on the wall buzzed. It was Clair, informing them that the car had arrived to take them to the airport. By the time it sunk in that Marc was suggesting he could buy her for two million he was already on the move and out of range of the tongue lashing he knew she wanted to unleash.

"Are you coming?" he asked.

With reluctance she followed.

Collecting the flight bag from where it had been left, Marc and Kate entered the lift and rode down to reception. The car was waiting for them outside.

Racing across London, they stopped at Kate's home briefly. Long enough for her to make a quick change from the jeans and skimpy t-shirt she was wearing into a traveling suit that would be comfortable on the journey, and to pack a few things in case she was forced to stay overnight.

While Kate was upstairs getting ready for the trip Marc had time to look around the house. It was a modest end-of-terrace in Southeast London and nothing at all like Marc's home which was decorated on a lavish, grand scale to designer level.

Kate's home was comfy. Marc was impressed with her taste in furnishing. There were contemporary art works on the walls, and some well-chosen pieces of furniture scattered about the place. On the whole the place was understated yet elegant.

From downstairs he called out to her. "Kate, while you're packing don't forget to throw in something pretty to wear. We're bound to go out for a meal. And knowing women, you'll want to change into something different."

"I'm sure you know women, but I don't intend to stay overnight in Paris," she called back. "As soon as I've found Nikki I'll be leaving. We'll be catching the next flight back to England."

"I wouldn't be too sure about that. I suggest you pack something just in case." Marc wasn't sure if she would take his advice, but he hoped she did.

With her passport in hand and an overnight bag packed Kate was at last ready to leave England.

"Are we ready?" Marc asked, glancing at his watch.

"As ready as I'll ever be. I hope you realize I'm an unwilling traveler and would have much preferred to remain here in London. But if I'm to find Nikki and bring her home safe and unscathed, I suppose I'll have to fly to Paris with you."

"Think of this as an adventure, Kate. Our first adventure together."

Journeying through London's heavy traffic toward Heathrow Airport was done in typical Castell fashion—at high-speed and in style.

Unlike most people, when Marc got to the airport there was no waiting at passport control points or in the VIP lounge for him. The limousine went unchecked, straight through the security check-in barrier to a private hanger where his Lear jet was housed.

Hal had already carried out Marc's orders, and with the plane fueled and on stand-by, it was ready for take-off.

As they pulled into the hanger a black Range Rover was following hard on their tail. Throughout their journey from Castell House to the airport it had been there, tracking them through the streets of London, like a silent shadow all the way. Several bodyguards were in the Range Rover, and they had been keeping a discreet surveillance distance ever since Marc had left headquarters.

Usually, Marc didn't travel with full-on security protection. It was only when he was in Europe or taking an international trip somewhere that a security detail was dispatched to travel with him. The entourage was mostly for show. But after an incident a few years ago, when there had been an attack on his life, precautions and safety measures had been put into place, and it was decided that security guards were a necessity and they couldn't be avoided.

A man such as Marc Castell, a man who was worth billions of dollars, was always going to be at risk, and that was something Marc had to live with. Having bodyguards present acted as a deterrent to those with harmful intentions, and there were plenty of people out there who, given the opportunity, would take advantage of Marc if he let them, but he never did.

With the jet fueled and ready to go, take-off was almost immediate, and in no time at all they were on their way to Paris.

During the flight Marc wasn't idle. On several occasions he'd been to the cockpit to talk with Hal, and when he returned to his seat it wasn't to waste his time watching a movie on the flat screen, it was to continue working, using his laptop.

His original intention was to use the flight time to become better acquainted with his captive audience, Kate, but it wasn't to be.

He had a backlog of work to get through, and now that the Italian meeting was on hold there was a lot to reorganize. Agendas, schedules, and meetings required reshuffling to accommodate altered plans, and although the chance of making conversation with Kate on the flight was sparse, he knew that if he got organized now it would free up some of his valuable time, time he could spend with her later.

It was obvious to everyone that Marc was a workaholic, and he was also a man with no time for a serious, meaningful relationship. He was an ambition driven businessman and a jet-setting playboy; it was a lethal combination. He worked hard and played hard, and without shame he reaped the rewards and benefits from both activities.

Whenever he chose to unwind there was usually some lucky lady on hand to cater to his needs, but those brief, casual relationships were often short-lived, and they never lasted. Inevitably he moved on before things became too serious, and in his wake he always left a trail of expensive thank you gifts. The gifts were mementos for favors given, and when a woman received one of the extravagant, overgenerous presents, she knew her time with Marc was over.

With his money Marc was lavish to a fault—with his love...never.

His main passion was his work, and it was the one thing he could be sure of. Since his experience with Agnés, women had shown him that he couldn't count on the female sex. He found their needs and desires could change from one moment to the next. One minute they wanted him physically, and the next...he soon discovered they wanted only a good time and all the material things he could lavish on them.

No...work was the only thing he knew and trusted. And work was the only thing he lived for.

* * * *

With the flight underway Kate realized it was about time she made a long overdue phone call to Patty.

Patty was a female version of a right-hand man and was also the top assistant at McKenna Catering. She was in charge, holding down the fort, while Kate was running around chasing after Eduardo Castell.

It had been a couple of hours since Kate had checked in to make sure today's booked events were going according to plan, so she decided that now was the best time to give Patty a call.

Kate always liked to know that everyone involved with McKenna Catering was happy. Running a business was quite a responsibility, but she knew that if she was to make her way in the catering world she would have to accept some sort of accountability, and looking after her staff was part of it.

Owning a catering firm came at a price. With responsibilities and deadlines to meet Kate couldn't take time off from her business whenever she felt like it. McKenna Catering wasn't a nine-to-five job. She always had to be on call and make herself available for anyone who wished to speak with her. But today had been an exception. Today she'd been concentrating solely on Nikki. Work had been put on hold while she'd chased after her errant sister.

Phoning Patty to explain she was on a flight bound for Paris and that she wouldn't be back to work that day was something she knew she had to do. And when she did finally get through to her office it was reassuring to hear everything at McKenna Catering was going without a hitch. They were on schedule and tomorrow's orders and bookings had already come in and were being processed.

"Don't worry about us," Patty said cheerfully. "We'll be fine. You've got things so organized here that the ship could almost run itself. And you know Nikki always lands on her feet. Take as long as you like, Kate. Enjoy yourself while you're in Paris.

There's no need to rush back to London, and who knows...perhaps you'll find a man who'll be willing to take you for a meal. Someone to whisk you off your feet, give you a romantic night out, and show you the city made for lovers."

"I'm not here to be wined and dined by a man," Kate said, shocked by Patty's suggestion. "I'm not here to find some handsome, French, seducing gigolo who's looking for a one-night stand."

As soon as Kate said those words she felt hot, cringing waves of shame and embarrassment wash over her. It was unbelievable, but for some reason she'd forgotten who was sitting next to her.

There was an awkward moment when she realized she could have been describing Marc to a "T", and more than likely he was probably thinking the same; that she was indeed talking about *him*.

Could he really think she'd been talking about him? She turned her head in Marc's direction to gauge his reaction, and she caught a dark, disparaging look in his eyes. Obviously he did think that.

"Maybe the man you meet will take you to Tiffany's. Give you breakfast and—"

"Goodbye, Patty," Kate said somewhat dryly as she pressed the *disconnect* button on her cellphone, ending the call.

Marc continued to look questioningly at Kate.

"Don't ask," she warned him. "Don't even go there."

She was sure that the sudden flare of her temper and the heated blush on her cheeks told him that the call had ended on a somewhat embarrassing note.

"Gigolo!" was all he said with a glint of humor shining in his eyes, and then he looked away, turning his attention back to the laptop's computer screen.

All too soon it was time for them to fasten their safety belts, and the plane started its descent. Touchdown at de Gaulle airport was faultless. They had arrived in Paris.

After the plane coasted into a private hanger Kate and Marc were met by several airport officials who escorted them into the terminal. They were taken straight past customs and were led outside to a waiting limo.

"We'll go to the hotel and see what's happening," Marc said as he sank back into the soft, cushioned leather seats of the car.

He looked relaxed, as if he was preparing to enjoy the passing scenery, but Kate couldn't relax, at least not until she knew where her sister was. She wouldn't be able to rest until she set eyes on Nikki.

"Is there any news? Do you know where Nikki is?" she asked, anxious to know the worst.

"She's safe. Don't worry," he said almost indifferently.

"But she could be anywhere in Paris, or anywhere in France."

"We don't have to find her," he told her. "I know exactly where Nikki and Eduardo are and what they're doing. Detectives have been following them since they landed about an hour ago. During our flight, reports were coming through to the jet's cockpit, and Hal kept me updated."

"So you know where they are?"

"Of course I know. They've already booked into the Paris hotel—The Castell Plaza. It seems they're planning to stay in one of our luxury suites."

"They're sharing the same room?"

"Not if I have anything to do with it."

"But what if they..." Her voice faltered. She was sounding almost desperate.

"What if they...what?" he asked, waiting for her to make her meaning quite clear.

"You know what I mean," she said, reluctant to say the actual words. Surely she didn't have to spell it out to him.

"No, I don't know what you mean. Explain it to me. What is it that I'm supposed to know?"

Marc was being deliberately obtuse. He knew exactly what Kate meant, but for some reason he was teasing her.

Kate looked to the front of the car where the chauffeur was sitting and was thankful the partition screen was up. The screen made it impossible for the driver to overhear their conversation.

"What if they take the next step?" she whispered. "What if they take the next step and sleep together?" There...she'd said it. She'd said the very thing she hadn't wanted to voice.

"So that's what they're calling *sex* these days...the next step. Well, let me tell you, they won't be taking the next step under my roof." Marc sounded as if he was sure of this fact. There was determination behind his words. "I've told the hotel team to babysit them. The staff will be in and out of their suite so many times they won't have a chance to breathe let alone indulge in any *pleasurable pastimes.* At least not the sort you seem to have in mind."

"You mean you have someone there to keep an eye on them? You're watching them?"

"I've left strict instructions your sister is at no time to be alone in the suite with my nephew. If I have any say in the matter, she won't have a chance to get her claws into him."

Hearing Marc say those words Kate relaxed...that was until she realized exactly what he was implying. Marc was suggesting that it was Nikki who was the villain in this affair. Did he really believe his nephew was the innocent party?

"How can you still think my sister and I are out to blackmail you?" she asked crossly. "We don't need your money, and I can assure you we wouldn't take it from you even if you offered it to us."

Marc shrugged. "I'm not taking any chances. This time there'll be no possibility of blackmail or threats of any kind."

"This time?" Kate asked, wondering what he meant.

"You don't need to know all the sordid details of our family's complex love affairs. And sometimes it's best if things are left unsaid, especially if it concerns Eduardo's previous entanglements in love. They are nothing to do with you. But weighing up all the facts, even though you seem like a charming person, more than likely you and Nikki have got some sort of scheme planned." His frustration was obvious. "I need to get to the bottom of things. I need to know what's happening between Eduardo and Nikki, but more importantly, I want to know to what extent you are involved in this fiasco?"

"What makes you so certain we're planning something, or that I'm involved?"

Marc threw back his head and laughed, but it wasn't a pleasant laugh. "To start with...you've made several threats," he said, taking the plunge and confronting her.

"Did I? And what threats were those?" She had no idea what Marc was talking about.

"You threatened to go to the authorities," he reminded her. "You also said you're going to make Eduardo pay for any harm he causes Nikki."

Thinking about it, Kate knew Marc was right. She had said those things. But that was because she'd thought Eduardo meant to use Nikki and break her heart. For all she knew that might still be true.

"If it's not money you're after, it will be marriage," Marc said cynically, shrugging and lifting his hands upward in a typical French gesture. "All I know is something's telling me to watch my back and guard what's mine. And that's what I'm about to do."

"It's not about your money...or marriage," she protested. "I would never blackmail you, and I'd never insist that Eduardo marries Nikki."

"You might not know it but there's more than one way to use extortion for gain."

"Such as?" she asked, challenging him.

"All it would take would be one night of passion and there could be...*consequences*."

"Consequences? I'm not sure I know what you mean," she said hesitantly, but she knew exactly what Marc was suggesting. He was suggesting Nikki would use sex and the possibility of conceiving a child with Eduardo to her advantage. Kate fought to control the agitated rise and fall of her breasts as anger overcame her.

"You're not that naïve, Kate. And you pretending to be makes me speculate all the more. I'd like to know what you're hoping to gain from the Castell family." Marc gave her a long, hard look.

"I want nothing from you...nothing. Not even a kiss."

And those words were Kate's undoing. As soon as she said them, Marc reached over and placed an arm tightly around her waist. He pulled her up against him, and as he trapped her against his side he pushed her back into the deep softness of the limousine's leather seating. Suggestively, he began playing with the fastenings on her blouse.

Kate gasped. His sudden surprise attack had caught her off guard, and tingles of sexual arousal were awakening deep within.

The back of Marc's hand slipped beneath the fabric of her blouse, and with slow, caressing motions he began stroking her flesh. She was on fire. His touch did that to her. He had her panting for breath, and against her will he was awakening dormant desires within her. As Marc pinned her down with his weight into the corner of the limo, her pulse beat faster. There was no way she could escape the erotic touch or sensual feel of his seeking hands. And she didn't want to.

Cornered, she lay defenseless in his embrace. "What are you doing?" she asked breathlessly. "What is it you want from me?"

"I want more than just a kiss from you," he said, teasing her. "I could be about to offer you something you can't refuse."

"You have nothing I want," she told him, knowing she was lying.

There was plenty she wanted from him. She wanted the feel of his hands never to stop touching and caressing her. She wanted him to do things to her no one had ever done before. But most of all, she wanted him to need her like she needed him...now.

"So..." he said in a soft, seductive whisper against her ear as they drove through the rush-hour traffic of Paris. "What do you think *our next step* ought to be?"

He kissed the exposed skin of her arched neck before plundering her trembling lips and mouth. His deep, long, tender kisses left her fighting for air, and she struggled for breath, and the ability to retain her sanity. He was driving her crazy, and she wanted more of him.

"I don't know," she mumbled, clutching in desperation at the lapels of his jacket for support. "I don't know what our next step should be."

"Well, I do," he said, and once again his mouth found hers.

CHAPTER FOUR

As the sleek, black limousine pulled into the forecourt of the Castell Plaza Hotel Marc reluctantly broke his hold on Kate, then reached out and smoothed a stray lock of her hair back into place. He was frustrated that their journey had ended so soon.

A doorman was standing at the ready, waiting to help the two occupants get out of the limousine. The man discreetly averted his gaze as Marc placed yet another long, lingering kiss on Kate's lips.

"It seems we'll have to postpone our next step," Marc murmured softly.

Getting out of the limo, Marc walked around the car and joined Kate on the forecourt. Taking her by the arm, he led the way toward the hotel. At the entrance to the hotel were two large revolving doors, and having crossed the extravagant length of the luxurious lobby, Marc and Kate made their way to reception.

The Castell Plaza Hotel was a building of large proportions, and the colossal size of everything about them was impressive. There was also an amazing number of staff hovering near reception.

It appeared word had spread that Marc Castell—owner and company director—was on his way, and anyone who could find a legitimate reason or an opportunity to be in the lobby was there watching and waiting for his arrival. Everyone was eager to assist the VIP party from England. A porter immediately collected their bags and left to take them upstairs to their rooms.

As Marc and Kate made their way through the hotel to the penthouse Marc got the impression Kate was stunned by the opulence of the place. Crystal chandeliers hung from the ceiling. Large Persian rugs were lying scattered on the tiled marble floor between seating areas, and there were gleaming gilded mirrors and decorative silk fabrics covering the walls.

Castell Plaza Hotel was a five-star *plus* hotel, and the place did indeed look like a palace.

Following Marc's orders, no expense had been spared on the recently refurbished interior of the hotel. Every comfort for its array of cosmopolitan guests had been catered for, and here in the hotel, extravagance and indulgence were the key words.

Moving toward the lifts, Marc placed an arm around Kate's waist. He was claiming her. Everyone who saw them together was being made aware of the fact that Kate was with him. The physical contact between them as she walked beside him was stirring his senses once again. Her scent was teasing his nostrils and...he wanted to possess her.

Once in the lift they went straight to a rooftop apartment which covered the whole of the south-facing side of the building. It overlooked the Golden Triangle, a district of Paris, and gave clear views of the *Champs-Élysées* and beyond.

The penthouse suite was always held in reserve for Marc's personal use twenty-four-seven, and when he traveled to Paris on business, which was often, the penthouse was his base. Only if he was elsewhere in the world and he wasn't expected to arrive in Paris anytime soon were his friends and relatives permitted to use his private suite. Knowing Marc's wishes, management had given Eduardo and Nikki no access to his suite of rooms.

Once Marc and Kate were inside the sprawling apartment the porter asked in a diplomatic way, "May I enquire if there is any particular room you would like *Madam's* bags to be left in, sir?"

Marc got the message. The porter wanted to know if they would be sharing the bedroom.

"Miss McKenna and her sister will be having the use of the penthouse, and I'll move to another suite for the duration of their stay in Paris," he said offhandedly.

Marc could see Kate was about to protest the fact that he was giving up his penthouse for her, but when she caught the look of warning in his eyes, she remained silent. Just in time he'd stopped Kate from saying something in front of the porter. The less said, the less likelihood there was of a scandal spreading about the hotel concerning this whole disastrous affair.

"You can put Miss McKenna's luggage in my room, Gérard, and see that her sister's belongings are transferred to *de crème chambre*."

"Yes, sir."

Having placed Kate's overnight case in Marc's room, Gérard returned to the lounge and stood near Marc's bag, awaiting instructions.

"Please inform my nephew and Miss Nikki McKenna of our arrival. Tell them they are both expected to join us for dinner downstairs in about…" Marc looked at his watch then back at Gérard. "An hour."

"Certainly. Will that be all, sir?"

"*Oui*, Gérard. *Merci*."

* * * *

And then Marc said something to Gérard in French.

He was speaking too quickly and fluently for Kate to understand what had been said. Her French was good, but not that good. Like most tourists she could make herself understood, but his instructions to

Gérard seemed complicated and too obscure for her to understand.

"*Oui, monsieur*." Gérard said before retrieving Marc's luggage and leaving the room.

Once again they were alone.

Walking over to one of the large sofas Marc, without ceremony, plonked himself down. "Come and join me," he said, patting the vacant place beside him.

The sofa looked very comfortable, but Kate ignored his offer. "I'd prefer to go in search of Nikki if you don't mind."

"She'll be all right. She's in the hotel."

"But I'd still like to see her."

"And so you shall. As soon as we get our story straight," he said, his jaw clenched with determination.

"Story? What story?"

"The one I'm going to tell you to tell Nikki. Now be a good girl and come here." Once again he patted the cushion. "I dislike having to shout across the room."

"Don't tell me what to do, and I'm not your girl, and there's no story to get straight," she said as her eyes locked with his in battle.

"I'm sorry," he said, obviously realizing that he'd ruffled her feathers. "Of course you're quite right. You don't need to be told anything."

Eventually Kate walked over, and joined him on the sofa. Instantly, she knew that it was the wrong move for her to have made. All Marc had to do was stretch out his hand and he could touch her, but thankfully, he didn't.

"How old is your nephew?" she asked, curious to know more about Eduardo. "I think I ought to discover at least something about him before we meet, don't you? Things like...what type of person is he? What are his interests? And where does Nikki come into the picture?"

"Umm..." Marc said thoughtfully. "I guess he'd be about twenty...twenty-one. And as far as I know he has no interests, or at least he shouldn't have. Work and earning a living should be the only thing he has on his mind. As for Nikki...well, I have no idea how she features in his life."

"Actually," Kate said as she turned on the sofa to look him squarely in the eye. "I have a bit of a confession to make. When I walked into your office looking for him and found you, it was a shock to say the least. I was surprised, and having taken one look at you I thought Nikki was being chased by an older man."

"So I'm an *older* man, am I?"

"You know what I mean," she said.

"Were you disappointed that I wasn't Eduardo?"

"What do you mean...disappointed?"

Marc rephrased the question. "Are you *relieved* I'm not Eduardo?"

"I don't know. I haven't met him. As yet I've no comparison with which to make, but if you're anything to go by, I'm not sure I should relax my guard. He could be even more of a womanizer than his uncle. To be truthful, at the moment I'm not inclined to trust you or your nephew."

Marc chuckled, but his amusement only fueled her temper.

"You Castells are probably all the same," she said on a caustic note. "You're all flirts, cheats, and...playboys."

Marc threw back his head and let out a tremendous roar of laughter, which only infuriated Kate even more.

"A flirt maybe, a cheat perhaps, but a playboy...never."

He'd taken her scathing comments on the chin.

"I know you have a reputation," she said crossly. "But I hadn't realized it was a reputation for being unintelligent, dim-witted, and obtuse."

"Look..." he said, ignoring her biting remarks. "I can assure you Eduardo is harmless, and by running off together those two have already made their point. The young lovebirds think they're in love. They've come to Paris, the city of romance, with the intention of being together. Perhaps that's all it is...they might just want to be with one another and we're reading more into the situation than there is."

"What do you mean?" she asked, perplexed.

"I've been thinking...when you first told me about them going away together I didn't want to get involved, but I was willing to put a stop to their affair because you were so adamant that that was what was needed. But I think I've changed my mind. It's now my belief that if we try to separate them it will only cause trouble."

"They shouldn't be left alone," Kate protested. She was determined to make her position on the matter clear. She was trying to defend and keep Nikki's innocence intact.

"There's nothing we can do," he said, stressing the point. "If we forbid them to see one another...next time we might not be so lucky."

"What do you mean *next time*?" Kate asked, shocked to the core.

"To be honest, I think if Eduardo had meant to have a *casual affair* with Nikki he would have taken her to some out-of-the-way hotel in England. He wouldn't have come to Paris only to flaunt her under the nose of my staff. He would know that news of his activities would reach me."

"You mean that's what you would do? You would go to a cheap hotel where no one knows you and have a weekend fling with someone?"

"I didn't say cheap, and I might do just that...if I were his age and in his shoes. But I'm not."

"Am I to understand that because we're not in London you think Eduardo might be serious?" Kate asked.

"He wouldn't have brought her to Castell Plaza where everyone knows him if he wasn't."

* * * *

Kate was in a rage but Marc couldn't fathom the workings of her mind. He didn't know what he'd said that was so offensive.

"What's worrying you now?" he asked.

Obvious displeasure was written all over Kate's face. "Do you think you've put my mind at ease? Well, let me assure you...you haven't. On the contrary, I'm anything but relaxed."

"Then tell me what's wrong." He waited patiently for Kate to explain.

"Nothing's wrong," she told him, and then, as if unable to stop herself, she continued. "Well, if I'm honest, everything's wrong. From the moment I left the house this morning everything has conspired against me. I'm here in France, a place where I hadn't expected to be, and don't particularly want to be, and I'm with a man who is demanding, overbearing, and bossy. But that's not the worst of my troubles. To top it off, you expect me to be thankful Eduardo thinks enough of Nikki to bring her to Castell Plaza and not some sleazy hotel. If you think that's supposed to reassure me about his character, you're mistaken."

Marc was beginning to understand what triggered Kate and why she was genuinely distressed about her sister's relationship with his nephew.

"Kate, you're too defensive, almost overly protective when it comes to your sister. You're like a mother hen fussing with her chick. It's time to let her grow up. Eduardo's young. He's finding his footing with women, and I'm not going to put a damper on his *amorous* adventures. But I must admit, having had time to think, I don't believe Eduardo considers Nikki to be an amorous adventure."

"My sister is definitely not an *amorous adventure*. But that doesn't stop me from thinking it's not good for them to be left alone together," she said, enraged.

"Let me reassure you they haven't been alone for any length of time, and they won't be. Not on my watch. They'll be under constant surveillance...at all times."

"But will that be enough?" she asked.

"It will have to be."

Marc could see Kate had yet to be convinced they were doing the right thing in regard to Nikki and Eduardo. She wanted to shield Nikki from the likes of his nephew, but from an outsider's perspective, Marc didn't think Nikki needed protecting.

"You know, Kate, it seems to me you're still keen to keep them apart, whereas I'm beginning to think it would be better if we let the romance fade naturally. They'll soon tire of one another. All young lovers fall out of love, and when that happens they'll go their separate ways." There was almost an uncaring note of cynicism in his voice.

"But that could take months," she said.

"It could. But knowing Eduardo, if he's not serious he'll soon move on to the next girl."

"Oh, great," she said, exasperated, and thumped a conveniently placed cushion that was beside her on the sofa. "I'll be the one who has to pick up the shattered pieces of my sister's broken heart. I'm telling you *Mr. Know-It-All Marc Castell*, you can't let this happen. You have to intervene before it's too late."

Marc began thoughtfully mulling over his options, and after some consideration he decided to do as Kate asked. But only because he knew that now was the time to make his move and deliver his ultimatum.

"All right, I'll intervene," he said with some reluctance. "But on one condition."

"And that condition is..."

Unsuspecting, Kate had fallen into his trap. And she had no idea what she was letting herself in for.

"The condition is you come away with me for the remainder of the weekend."

"Away with you? This weekend?" she asked, amazed and confused. "Do you mean *this* weekend. But that's impossible. We're in Paris. We're here to deal with Nikki and Eduardo. And why would I want to go away with you, and where would we go?"

Marc didn't answer immediately. He was giving her time to process what he'd said.

"Here's the deal," he said coolly, and then he rolled back the sleeves of his shirt and began getting down to business. "I believe I've gotten to know you...a little. You seem like a person of good character with high morals, and you might even have some integrity. I'm prepared to give Nikki the benefit of the doubt in the hope that, like her sister, she too has an honorable nature. Either way, I'm prepared to think the best and give her a chance...at least for now."

"A chance?"

"Yes. I'll allow her to see Eduardo, and I'll assume she's not after his money. In return all I'm asking from you is that you also give Eduardo a chance. Let them get to know one another. Let them take things at their own pace. Make their own mistakes. But most of all, you're not to interfere."

"What right do you have to say you'll *allow* Nikki to see Eduardo? Only someone who is supremely arrogant and egotistically obnoxious would dare say such a thing. And interfere! I never interfere in the things Nikki chooses to do...at least not in the way you're suggesting."

Having heard his offer Kate was becoming enraged. Marc ignored her outburst and continued.

"Castell Plaza staff can chaperone them while they're here exploring Paris. That means you and I will be free to leave for Cannes...tomorrow morning."

"Cannes? Why Cannes?" she asked.

"When we were in London do you remember I asked you what you were prepared to do to get your sister back safe and sound?"

"Vaguely," she said. "Where are you going with this? What is this leading up to?"

"You said you were willing to do anything in return for my help. Remember?"

"I asked you to stop Eduardo before it was too late."

"They're here in the hotel, and as far as I know nothing's happened, but anything could still happen if I withdraw the watchful eyes of my staff. Eduardo could...well, Eduardo could do whatever he liked. Go anywhere he liked, and be with anyone of his choosing. *Night and day.* So let me ask you again...what are you prepared to do to keep your sister safe? Are you prepared to keep your word and come with me to Cannes?"

Marc was using Kate's demons against her. Apart from the fact he was still unsure if the

McKennas were out to get the Castell fortune or not, in truth, he wasn't concerned with Eduardo and Nikki anymore, but he knew Kate was. And that was what he was going to use against her.

In return for Nikki's safety he was going to make Kate promise to help him in any way he chose during their time together in Cannes.

* * * *

Kate couldn't believe what Marc was asking her to do.

"When I said I'd do *anything* I didn't mean *that,* and I don't see how my accompanying you to Cannes can help the situation between Nikki and Eduardo."

"It doesn't help them. It will help *me*."

"You?" she asked, mystified.

"Yes. I need an escort. A buffer. Someone to act as a shield against a woman I know. Your suggestion of taking a girlfriend to Cannes was brilliant, and as I need someone to pretend to be my girlfriend, or better still my lover, I thought you could help me out."

"Lover?" she said, aghast.

Stunned and alarmed, Kate stared at him in disbelief, and as she did so, she saw a slow smile of pleasure begin to appear on Marc's face. She was appalled at the thought he was imagining them as lovers.

"Don't sound so surprised," he said, amused at her obvious unease. "I said *act as my lover*. I didn't say be my lover. But on second thought, perhaps being my lover would solve our problem."

A glint of humor showed in Marc's dark eyes, and in one graceful move he lifted his arm and placed it along the back of the sofa, resting it dangerously near her head. The tips of his fingers began to stroke, teasing the curves of her exposed neck. Startled by his caressing touch, she edged cautiously away.

"I could never be your lover," she told him with a defiant toss of her chin.

"Never say never," he warned, a provocative smile on his lips. "Be advised, Kate, I like a challenge, and now it seems I shall have to persuade you otherwise."

Kate heard the loaded, seductive threat behind his words, and she didn't know if he was sincere about being lovers or not, but she couldn't take the chance.

The chase was on. He was in hot pursuit, and then seeing the intense look of desire in his eyes, she knew he was perfectly serious.

"You can't persuade me," she told him, determined to stand her ground. "I won't go with you. And nothing you say can make me enter into the pretense of being your girlfriend."

She hoped she'd made herself clear. She wanted nothing to do with Marc Castell and any relationship he might offer—real or unreal. But she was certain he wasn't accustomed to being denied anything or anyone, and suspected her refusal would probably only make the hunt and the winning of his prey that much more interesting.

"Are you sure?" he asked with a raised brow.

"Yes, I'm sure."

A dimple appeared at the corner of his mouth, and she knew that if he pushed her, it would be hard to resist his charm. Desperate, she searched for a plausible excuse, any excuse, to put Marc off. She had to find a reason to deter him. She needed to stop him from forcing her to go to Cannes with him, and recklessly Kate said, "I'm seeing someone."

There...she'd blurted it out. She'd lied...sort of.

"I don't see a ring," he said, looking at her ringless fingers.

Kate didn't have a steady boyfriend and she wasn't in a relationship, but she needed to give Marc the impression she was. He had to believe she was unavailable.

"Daniel and I have been seeing one another *umm*...for a while."

What she'd said wasn't a total lie. In a way it was sort of true. She did see someone named Daniel daily. Only Daniel wasn't her boyfriend. He was an employee. He drove one of her supply vans and took the catered food her company produced to events and functions. He was middle-aged, happily married, and had at least three teenage children that she knew of. He was the first person she could think of, and now that she'd claimed him as a boyfriend she didn't know how long she could maintain the deception.

She wanted Marc to think it would be wrong for her to go away with him on the spur of the moment, and a boyfriend had been the only solution she could think of. She knew that eventually she would say something and give the game away, but until then if Marc thought she was already taken, she might be safe from any amorous onslaughts he made.

"All right. Let's say you have a serious boyfriend, which I doubt, that doesn't stop you from coming to Cannes with me. That is unless he's not man enough to trust you."

"Daniel trusts me," she said.

"Then what's stopping you?" Marc raised his brows questioningly.

Curiosity got the better of Kate. She couldn't resist. She had to ask. "Who's this woman you want to avoid?"

Marc smiled, and she realized Marc had seen a chink in her armor. She'd shown her interest, and she was weakening to his needs. "It doesn't matter who she is. She might not make a move. For now all that you need to know is that I need you with me. I need someone to be a barrier and act as a deterrent. You being with me ought to achieve that."

Kate made a noise that sounded like a scoff. "I'm sure you can handle any woman on your own. You don't need me."

"That's where you're wrong," he persisted. "It's a delicate situation. If Cade's wife should find her way into my bed..."

"Cade?" she asked, puzzled.

"Yes. My accountant…but more importantly, my friend."

Kate disliked the thought of someone's wife jumping in and out of another man's bed, especially Marc's bed. It didn't matter that she didn't know these people; she believed nothing should ruin a good friendship—but then perhaps this wasn't a good friendship.

"I need you there," he said.

Marc was supposed to be a man in control of his own destiny, but at this moment Kate thought he sounded nothing like a man in charge of his own fate.

"It's madness. Impossible. I don't know you, and I don't know what you'd expect of me," she said.

Marc stood up and moved away, giving her some breathing space, but returning to the sofa, he leaned in and whispered softly in her ear, "Then get to know me."

There was a hungry determination hidden behind his words. His hand caressed her cheek. His touch was electrifying. It always was. Whenever Marc brushed against her she always reacted. She had to. Her body had a mind of its own, and she couldn't resist.

"I'm sorry, Marc, I can't. I have to get back to England. I have a business to run, and my schedule's full. I can't take time off just because you want me to."

"If you want to achieve something in life, sometimes you have to make sacrifices."

Frantic, she searched for a reason to back out of the unsuspecting promise she'd made, and feeling pressured, she sought in desperation for an excuse not to stay. Emotionally, she was being pulled in two directions. Torn between the need to help her sister and the urge to run from Marc, she couldn't decide what was for the best. Then Kate realized she couldn't fight his irresistible charm and persuasion any longer. The battle was over, and she had to make a choice…but this? Surely he was asking too much from her?

"You know that if I do go with you I can't be your girlfriend…*or lover*." She was caving in, panicking, and some of the thoughts racing through her head came blurting out. "Marc, it wouldn't work. We're from different worlds. No one would believe we were together or that we are an item. They wouldn't believe a successful billionaire would pick an insignificant person like me to be with."

Had she really said those words out loud? Was she really considering his suggestion? And then she realized Marc had already won the battle. She was thinking of them as a couple and imagining them together, as lovers.

Leaning down toward her, Marc took her face gently between his strong hands and looked deep into her eyes. "You're not an insignificant person, Kate. Never let me hear you say that again. You are Kate McKenna and you will be with me. You will be *my Kate*."

Strolling over to the drinks table, Marc began pouring a stiff whisky, and as he did so she was given time to consider her options. She was aware Marc was a master of strategy and that he knew when to pursue and when to retreat from his prey. Without her being aware of him doing so, he had gradually, and ever so carefully, let out a line, knowing that eventually it would be reeled in and she would be hooked. She would be caught, mesmerized in his power, and he would pounce.

"Would you like something to drink?" he asked, indicating an array of decanters on a tray.

She shook her head, declining his offer.

He persisted. "Sherry? A soft drink perhaps?" When he saw her hesitate he opened the mini-bar and poured a cool, refreshing, soft drink before she could refuse.

While Marc was busy with the drinks Kate had a chance to look around the room. It was luxurious to the extreme in its design. It was a masculine room. Definitely a man's domain, with no frills or flounces visible. Contemporary landscape paintings hung on the walls, depicting various locations in France, but the one painting that caught her eye, drawing her back to look more closely at it, was a seascape view showing a sleepy, seaside harbor with yachts moored along a sun-drenched quayside. There was also a house, a modern building with a crisp, white exterior tucked into the hillside above a sandy beach.

Before Kate could ask Marc about the painting he'd brought the drink he'd been making over to her.

"Thank you," she said, and reached for the glass.

Ice tinkled against the sides of the chilled tumbler, and as she took it from his hand their fingers touched. She froze. It only took the briefest caress of his burning fingers to shatter her composure. Her senses soared and there was instant sexual tension between them.

"I've got a proposition for you," he said offhandedly, almost carelessly, as if unconcerned what response she would give. "I'm going to ask you to spend one night with me. Just one night. We'll be in Cannes for two days, and while we're there I'd like to create an illusion of being in a real relationship...with you."

"With *me*?"

"Yes. All I want is one night of your company. I'll speak to Eduardo and I'll make him promise never to see Nikki again. Is one night with me too much to ask in exchange for saving your sister's innocence?"

Kate couldn't believe what she was hearing. Was Marc really saying he wanted her to spend one night with him in his bed? Did he really mean what she thought? Was he suggesting they have sex? Casual sex with any man was against all her principles, but as she looked at him standing there, towering over her, she saw he was serious. Although he hadn't actually said the words, she knew Marc wouldn't refuse or say no to a relationship on a more intimate level...even if it was only for one night.

But when she thought about it she realized he hadn't actually said anything about being intimate. All he'd asked was that she shared his bed for one night to make it seem they were in a relationship. It was up to her to figure out what he was suggesting, and it was up to her to figure out what she was willing to give.

"But you wouldn't want me to literally share your bed. Would you?"

"If you're to act as my girlfriend...yes, that is exactly what I would expect. If we start this illusion, I can't take the chance that people would discover it wasn't true and that you didn't sleep with me. Staff talk. It needs to look like you shared my bed and that we are lovers."

CHAPTER FIVE

Marc felt elated. He realized victory was within his grasp, and savoring his moment of triumph he watched with some delight as Kate struggled with her emotions. By now he thought he knew Kate well enough to know she would sacrifice almost anything or anyone to help her sister, including herself, and he was willing to play on that weakness.

What man wouldn't take advantage of the situation if he could have Kate in his bed?

Sex was exactly what Marc wanted and hoped for from Kate. He wanted her to share his bed and sleep with him, but he wasn't going to force her. She had to do it willingly.

"This is coercion," Kate said, enraged, as she glared at him. "What you're asking me to do is nothing but a threat."

If coercion was what it took to get her interested, then coercion was what he was prepared to use.

His gaze was steady, and as he looked into her troubled eyes he could see the battle of wills she was enduring. There was a spark of temper in their depths, and studying her more closely he liked what he saw. She looked feisty, determined, and she was radiating the sort of assertive energy he admired. Having observed her strength of character and seeing the way in which she fought for her sister, he'd come to a decision that he wouldn't mind having this woman on his team.

Kate would fight well in any battle she undertook, and if a man had her at his side, there would be a good chance they would win any crusade she was part of. He wanted her with him, and he was prepared to achieve his goal by fair or foul means.

"Not coercion," he said. "Call it an exchange of favors. You want me to do you a favor, and I'm asking for one in return."

"But I can't. I won't go with you," she protested, trying to stay calm. "What about my boyfriend? What about...umm...Daniel?"

Once again he joined her on the sofa and as he did Kate shifted, trying to avoid his nearness.

"What about him?" He had already dismissed Daniel as someone of no importance. If Daniel meant anything to Kate, they wouldn't be having this conversation.

"I can't go to Cannes with you," she told him again.

But he had the upper hand. Slowly but surely he was pulling her into his world. It was a world where jet-setting, high finance, and casual relationships were the norm.

"What's stopping you from coming with me, Kate?" he asked, and he was expecting an honest answer from her.

"I don't go to strange places with strange men," she told him candidly. "Before today we've never met. I don't know you. And I don't go to bed and have sex with strange men."

"What did you say?" he asked as he discovered Kate was assuming they were going to have sex.

"I said I don't have casual sex with strange men. It's not happening. We are not having sex. Is that clear?"

"Who said anything about sex?" he probed. "All I'm asking you to do is spend a night in my bed. But if you're offering your *services* as an extra...I might not refuse. In fact, I'm pretty sure I'd accept."

And they both knew exactly what he meant by *services*. Marc Castell, billionaire, hotel tycoon, and jet-setter had more or less said he was willing to have an affair, and Kate had fallen into his trap. She was open and exposed, and Marc planned to take full advantage of the situation.

"You mean you don't want to go to bed with me...*in that way*? You literally only want me to share your bed for the night?"

"Sort of," he told her truthfully. "You might not believe this, but I don't like or want *casual sex* either."

What he didn't say was that he wanted more from Kate. From the moment they met he knew she was someone special. He knew a jewel when he saw one, and for once he was willing to tread carefully.

Marc had never been in a serious relationship before. Of course he'd had love affairs, and plenty of them, but he'd always kept them brief. But with Kate, from the moment he'd first seen her in his office he sensed their relationship was going to be different. In fact, he needed it to be different. He'd decided he wanted more from her than a temporary relationship or a one-night stand. He wanted something lasting.

"Look," Kate said calmly. "The whole situation is impossible. We just met this morning, and I only agreed to come to Paris with you because I need to find Nikki. I need to make sure she's okay. I'm not here looking for a liaison with you or any other man. I haven't time to complicate my life with brief affairs. And hopping in and out of bed with anyone who happens to come along is out of the question. It's not my style."

"I'm glad to hear that." His voice was serious and he genuinely meant what he said. He was glad that she wasn't the type of woman who had casual one-night stands.

"I have to see Nikki," she told him again.

"Your sister's safe," he countered.

"I don't know that. She could be anywhere in Paris or anywhere in the world. I only have your word she's in this hotel."

"I promise you she is. Trust me. Your sister's safe...for now."

"It doesn't feel safe knowing Nikki's still with Eduardo. I don't know him. I've never met him. And you can't stop me from seeing her. If you do, I'll scream the place down."

"And if you're going to be difficult, I'll have you escorted off the premises." His tone of voice told her it was a warning and that he was on the point of getting tough.

"I suppose I can always phone the authorities," she threatened. "And when they come to the hotel I'll tell them you've kidnapped Nikki and they'll—"

"Do you think they'll believe you, *mon chère*? It's obvious that you have no idea how things work in Paris."

Meeting resistance from Kate, Marc was becoming increasingly annoyed, and as a result his French accent was becoming very pronounced.

Usually, whenever he made plans to get something done people obeyed instantly and without question. But Kate's defiance was trying his patience. He was beginning to wonder if he'd made an error and mistakenly judged Kate's character. Perhaps she wasn't the calm, level-headed person he thought her to be. Perhaps she wasn't the sort of person he ought to take to Cannes on this business trip.

* * * *

Kate was infuriated with the whole situation, and she didn't know if she should bash him on the nose or feel flattered by his proposal. But gradually she was beginning to see she had to make a choice. Marc had backed her into a corner, and she was beginning to realize she would have to give in to his preposterous demands.

"Suppose I do what you ask and travel to Cannes. What happens to Nikki?" she asked.

It seemed ridiculous to think she'd traveled all the way to France to rescue her sister only to leave her alone and at the mercy of Eduardo, once again. Nikki was on the brink of her first love affair, and as bad luck would have it, it happened to be with a Castell.

Even though Marc was assuring her Eduardo was harmless, Eduardo Castell sounded as if he was a ruthless heartbreaker...just like his uncle. After all, hadn't Eduardo persuaded Nikki to travel to France and wasn't Marc trying to persuade her to go to

Cannes? Thinking about it, Kate decided she couldn't and wouldn't trust any of the Castell men.

"I've already told you—nothing happens to Nikki. She'll have a good time in Paris and I'll see she's flown back safe to England."

Kate was uneasy about the whole situation. Marc was complicating her life with his plan, and it was a complication she didn't need.

"How do I know nothing bad will happen to her? What makes you think Eduardo will keep his hands to himself?"

"I can control Eduardo," Marc said in an unpretentious way. "He'll do as I say."

There was no hesitation or uncertainty as he spoke, and Kate believed him. She was in no doubt Marc could control anything or anyone he wished to. He had the ability and power to do anything he wanted. And if Marc was capable of handling anyone or anything in any given situation, she wondered why he needed her with him in Cannes.

"I can control Eduardo the same way I can control you." His voice was dispassionate, without expression. "With you I only have to touch you to make you do what I wish."

Then slowly, ever so slowly, he began to run his long, tapered fingers along her arm. The soft, sensual feel of his touch against her bare skin made her tremble. Against her will she responded to his caresses, and as he stroked her tenderly she couldn't help but quiver in anticipation.

"See?" he said. He had made his point. He had demonstrated his power over her.

Hurriedly, she pulled away from his hot, burning touch until she was out of range of his playful fingers. "And how do you plan to control Eduardo?" she asked bravely.

"With Eduardo it's not the heart strings but the purse strings that make him tick. Until he's twenty-five I control his allowance. He'll do whatever I tell him to do. If I say hands off Nikki, it's done."

"You told me you never get involved in your nephew's affairs."

"Normally I don't, but because you're asking me to protect your sister I'm prepared to bend my rule a little. So, what is it you want me to do? Do you want me to find an excuse to get Eduardo away from Nikki...or not? I can quite easily send him to Italy on some pretext or other."

"I need you to—"

Marc lifted his hand and stopped her in mid-sentence. "Before you tell me what you want I'm warning you whatever it is it comes at a price."

His voice was serious, and Kate realized she was about to make an important decision.

She knew Marc was a tough man when it came to business, and in some things he would be inflexible. He was the type that gave nothing away for free. That was the way he operated, and that was the way he had obviously achieved his success. Perhaps for a select handful of friends he might make an exception and bend his rules. But she wasn't a friend, and she certainly didn't think he would make allowances or grant her favors.

"And the price is?" Kate asked, waiting with baited breath for his reply.

"You know what the price is, Kate. It's Cannes and a night in my bed," Marc replied, his piercing eyes gazing into her own.

Her back was against the wall, and it was as if she was facing a firing squad. But she'd already made her position clear and told him she wasn't prepared to go to bed with him, at least not in that way. She knew she shouldn't become physically involved with him; it would be disastrous. He wasn't the type to have serious relationships. Going to bed with Marc would be nothing more than a one-night stand, and she didn't do one-night stands.

If Marc were to discover how vulnerable she felt when it came to men, especially when it came to him, she wouldn't survive.

Could she accept his terms and surrender? Could she sacrifice herself to save her sister? It was asking a lot, and she didn't know if she could overcome the emotional trauma she knew she would feel once she had given in to his demands and the weekend was over. She wondered if she would feel the same about herself. She had the feeling her life would never be the same again and that she would be forever changed.

Suspicious of Marc's motives and knowing he could have any woman he wanted, for a split second Kate wondered why he hadn't chosen someone else to take to Cannes. But it was only a brief, fleeting thought.

"You're despicable," she said, feeling deflated and defeated. She could feel the fight and energy draining from her. "I can't believe you would ask me to do something like this." Then, making one last attempt at defiance, she challenged him. "Do you think you can threaten me? Bargain with my body and make me do what you want?"

"It's your choice," he told her. "You can always refuse."

Putting on a brave face, Kate squared her shoulders and glared at him with what she hoped were daggers of contempt in her eyes.

"If using me against my will is what it takes to save Nikki's innocence...I'll do it. But on my terms." She had no other option. She had to do what he asked. "You can have me for one night and one night only, but after this weekend I never want to see you or hear from you again. You and Eduardo will be out of our lives. Gone. There will be no further contact between us. Do I make myself clear?"

"Fine," he said, and there was a glint of success shining in his eyes. "But I'm still going to try and persuade you otherwise."

"There's no use trying, Marc. I won't change my mind."

Kate felt defeated. Marc had stalked his prey and he'd won. She had conceded. She was going with him to Cannes and anything could happen during their weekend together.

"Tonight we'll stay in Paris, and tomorrow we'll leave for Cannes," he told her.

She felt as if her bridges had been burnt. She'd accepted his offer. She'd agreed to his demands and now she was his to command. Having reached the point of no return there was no going back. She'd gone beyond all her safe, familiar boundaries and now she was traveling into dangerous territory...and she would be traveling with Marc.

* * * *

Left alone in the hotel's penthouse Kate unpacked her holdall, snatched a few things up in her arms, and dashed to the bathroom. Having been on the go and traveling for most of the day across London and Europe, she'd become hot and sticky and felt the need to grab a refreshing shower before dressing for dinner.

Once showered and wearing a casual pair of dress trousers and a soft, creamy satin blouse, with her hair piled high in a chignon, she looked stylish and chic. She was ready to face an evening with Marc.

Entering the hotel's Michelin starred restaurant, which was situated in the basement of the building, Kate was escorted by a very efficient maître d' and shown to a table across the room where Marc, Eduardo, and Nikki were already seated.

It was obvious that a heated discussion was in progress. Although their voices were lowered, it was clear from the expressions on their faces that all was not well.

As Kate neared the table Marc stood and pulled out a chair for her.

"Sorry I'm a little late," Kate said brightly to everyone, trying to lighten the atmosphere. "But I'll have to blame Marc for my tardiness. All he said was to meet him in the restaurant downstairs, he didn't say which restaurant. I hadn't realized Castell Plaza has two restaurants from which to choose."

Marc passed a menu to Kate. "Yes, we're extremely fortunate," he said, taking her lead. "There's *The Grill Room* upstairs on street level. Passing customers can come in and eat without needing to book a table, and then there's our *Classic French Cuisine* restaurant which takes a reservation. Usually it's fully booked."

Nikki was playing nervously with her table place settings as she listened to Marc's explanation. She looked up and said, "Speaking of overbooking...I imagine Classic French Cuisine must be like the rest of the hotel. This afternoon Eduardo had great difficulty getting a room in his own hotel. He nearly caused a scene at reception. Reception told us there were only two single rooms available in the whole hotel. Not that we wanted a double. But nonetheless it seemed strange there were only two...and on separate floors. We couldn't have been placed further apart if it had been planned."

Marc looked at Kate and raised his brows knowingly, and Kate was left in no doubt he had taken precautions to keep them apart. Whatever his motives were for keeping her in the dark, she didn't care. She was just thankful that Nikki was safe and that the proficient staff on reception knew their job and had obeyed Marc's orders to the letter.

Eduardo squeezed Nikki's hand supportively, and looking at Marc and Kate he said, "You know there was no need for the two of you to follow us to Paris. I'm quite capable of taking care of Nikki. She wouldn't have come to any harm with me."

"That might be true," Marc said sternly to his nephew. "But Kate doesn't know that. And as Nikki's legal guardian she has every right to know where her charge is and with whom...at all times. You could be accused of kidnapping, and Kate can still press charges if she wishes to."

Eduardo looked crestfallen. "It wasn't my intention to—"

"Don't worry," said Kate reassuringly. She'd seen the look of genuine remorse on Eduardo's face. "No harm's been done, and Nikki's safe."

During the evening the atmosphere around the table gradually relaxed and conversation became general. At one point Marc explained Kate had offered to help him with business negotiations and was traveling with him to Cannes in the morning.

When Nikki and Eduardo heard of the plan they didn't seem at all surprised.

"That's great," Nikki said. "But I didn't realize you two had met before. Where did you meet?"

Anxious, Kate glanced at Marc with desperation in her eyes. She was worried Nikki suspected something unusual was happening, which of course it was. It wasn't in Kate's nature to go off for a weekend with a strange man, and Nikki knew that.

Kate thought that if her young sister started questioning further, perhaps the truth would have to be told, and that was something she didn't want to happen. Kate didn't want to reveal she was being blackmailed into sleeping with a man she'd only just met.

Slowly, Marc swirled the dark liquid in his wine glass, took a sip, and deflected the question. "On the plane traveling to Paris, Kate and I got to talking and I realized I need her. She's the ideal person to have with me, and I've persuaded her to accompany me this weekend. If things go according to plan, I intend to offer her a business contract." Marc looked at Kate and smiled as if he'd had a flash of inspiration.

Contract? What business contract? She had no idea what Marc was talking about, and she started to panic. What had she gotten herself into?

"I didn't know you were in the hotel business, Kate. What sort of contract is my uncle offering you?"

Kate couldn't answer Eduardo because she had no idea what Marc was talking about. Thankfully, Marc answered for her.

"I'd like to give McKenna Catering the opportunity to join Castell Hotels and Aniston Travel in a package deal we're offering our UK customers. I want Kate on my team."

"This is a new one on me," Eduardo said, surprised. "What's involved?"

"We need a caterer. Someone from outside the hotel. They're to provide some sort of packed lunch options for guests taking daytrips. That's where Kate's firm comes in. This weekend Aniston Travel is deciding if they're prepared to join Castell Hotels on this venture. If the deal goes through, I'd like for Kate to be in Cannes with me when the decision's made."

Even to Kate the explanation sounded plausible. But she knew in reality Marc would never offer her such a fantastic opportunity. This was make-believe. It was a dream contract. Every caterer's wish come true...and more. She also knew it wouldn't happen.

Her business in London was doing very well. It was expanding to such an extent that she knew McKenna Catering would be quite capable of filling such a magnificent catering contract, but she was realistic. In the real world billionaires such as Marc Castell never seriously made offers to firms such as McKenna Catering. This contract was too prestigious a project.

Marc would no more offer her such a venture than he would offer her a permanent relationship...or even marriage. No, this catering contract was a cover story. She was going to Cannes to be used as a shield for any romantic exploits that came his way...and packed lunch options for guests was a decoy.

"Who'll be there?" Eduardo asked curiously.

"Well, knowing Jeff and Robyn, they're sure to have some sort of party planned. There could be any number of people present. I know Cade and Yolanda Knightley are planning to show. Cade's there to sit in on the negotiations."

"Yolanda…she's Cade's wife?" Kate asked.

"Right."

"You mentioned he had a wife, but I didn't know her name." She looked at him and could read nothing from his expression. "I'm assuming she's not going to be there in a business capacity."

"Right again."

"So that means Yolanda's a tag-along, like me. She's the one you think might…"

One cold, unyielding stare from Marc was all it took to stop Kate in her tracks. Marc didn't say anything. He didn't have to, yet she knew she'd been warned. The subject of Yolanda was not open for discussion; especially not with Eduardo and Nikki within earshot.

Marc's silence said everything, and Kate's brain began working overtime. Visions of Marc and this unknown woman—Yolanda—were entering her head and they had her blushing with embarrassment as she imagined them making hot, steamy love.

"I expect everyone's going with their husband or wife," Nikki said with a knowing look in Kate's direction. "So I think it's great that Kate's tagging along with Marc. Don't you think so too, Eduardo? She'll be company for him, and he'll have someone at his side."

Secretly, Kate had hoped Nikki would oppose the idea of her going to Cannes with Marc. It would give her a valid reason to back out of her arrangement with him, but unfortunately no resistance came.

"I'll be with Marc on business," Kate was quick to explain. "We're not going to the Anistons for personal reasons. Otherwise, I'd be taking you home to England or you'd be coming with us to Cannes."

"Don't worry about me. I'm quite happy to stay with Eduardo. And I'm sure you and Marc will have a *great time*." There was a cheeky smile on Nikki's face as she gave Kate a knowing wink.

Kate was slightly agitated. Nikki had linked her with Marc as if they were a couple. And it was an impression she didn't want to give, to Nikki...or to anyone. One way or another it seemed fate and circumstances were working against her, but for now there was nothing she could do about it. It seemed she was destined to spend the weekend with Marc.

"I'm pleased you've decided you don't mind leaving Nikki with me," Eduardo said politely. "We'll be fine on our own. You'll see. And you can always call us on our cellphones and check to see if we're okay. But I expect we'll be out most nights this weekend and we won't get back to the hotel until late, so don't be surprised if you don't get an answer."

"I'm afraid that's not going to happen," said Marc with confidence while speaking to Eduardo. "I'm going to have to send you to Italy."

"What?" cried Nikki and Eduardo in unison. They looked at each other in dismay and then back to Marc in bewilderment.

Hearing that Eduardo and Nikki intended to be out at night frequenting bars and clubs, Kate had panicked. But when Marc decided it wasn't going to happen she felt nothing but a tremendous sense of relief. Listening to Eduardo's plans for the weekend she was sure, more than ever, that while she and Marc were in Cannes it would be best if Eduardo and Nikki were kept apart...at least for now.

"Yes," Marc said as he looked in Nikki's direction. "It's unfortunate, but we need some documents collected from Italy. I've given my word...I've made a solemn promise to someone that I would make sure Eduardo left Paris for Italy as soon as possible."

Marc glanced at Kate and she understood what he was telling her. She realized he meant to keep his word. He had promised her that if she spent a night with him he would see to it that Nikki's innocence was kept safe. And it seemed the only way to do that was to make sure that Eduardo and Nikki weren't together in the same city at the same time.

"This I do not believe," said Eduardo in amazement. It was clear that the thought of having to leave Nikki and Paris was causing him some alarm.

Marc took a deep sip from his wine glass and twirled the stem between his finger and thumb. The liquid danced in the soft candlelight before he returned the glass to its coaster.

"Eduardo, you're the only person I can entrust with the task of collecting the documents. Cade will be with us in Cannes. There's no one else available at the moment."

"Couldn't they send them to you by post or email?" Eduardo asked.

Kate knew Eduardo was trying to delay his departure, but she also knew that ultimately he would have to do what Marc asked. If Marc wanted something done, it had to be done...and without question. And in Kate's mind there was no doubt that tomorrow morning Eduardo would be on a plane bound for Italy and Nikki would either remain in Paris for what was left of the weekend or she would be returned to England.

During the remainder of the evening Kate came to realize Eduardo wasn't as much of a threat as she'd first imagined him to be. He was certainly not a ladies' man. He was a young, subdued man in his early twenties, and most of the time he appeared happy to follow Nikki's lead. He was more like an adoring puppy than a womanizing Lothario.

At one point during the evening, Marc and Eduardo excused themselves and went over to the bar to speak to someone. The two sisters were left alone, and Kate had taken the opportunity to tackle Nikki about coming to Paris with Eduardo. It was the first chance she'd had to question Nikki privately.

"What in the world made you come to Paris with Eduardo?" she whispered hurriedly. "He seems like a nice guy...but are you really considering having an affair with him?"

As soon as she'd asked the question she knew it had been the wrong thing to do and say. She was putting pressure on Nikki, and now was not the right time to go into the ins-and-outs of her relationship with Eduardo. Not here with the two Castell men within earshot.

"Don't be silly. At the moment Eduardo and I are just good friends...sort of. I like him *a lot* and he likes me—or at least I hope he does. We haven't really talked about our relationship and where it's going. For the moment we're here having fun, and having a good time...together. And for now, that's it. Anyway, I don't see what all the fuss is about. Most of my friends have boyfriends, and it's not like we're moving in together."

Kate was reassured by Nikki's answer, but she wasn't altogether satisfied. Anything could happen between the two, and she was glad Marc had made the decision to send Eduardo to Italy. For the time being Eduardo wasn't a problem, but Marc was another matter.

When Marc and Eduardo returned to their table Kate could tell by their smiles they were pleased with themselves about something.

"Sorry about that," Marc said as he sat down. Eduardo followed suit.

"That's all right," said Kate with a nonchalant shrug of her shoulders. "Nikki and I were catching up on gossip while you two were gone."

"I don't generally mix business with pleasure," Marc said. "But that was someone we've been trying to get a hold of for quite a while. He's selling some land next to one of our hotels, and I wanted to let him know I'm interested in purchasing it. It seems he's just returned from Hawaii."

"Grass skirts, coconuts, and white sandy beaches," interjected Eduardo wistfully, which resulted in a sharp dig in the ribs from Nikki.

"One-track mind…" Nikki said, shaking her head despairingly.

"What? What's wrong with white sandy beaches?" Eduardo laughed.

"I'm sure Eduardo doesn't mean anything by it," Kate said, and then she looked across the table at Marc. "But talking of grass skirts…I think before we leave for Cannes I need to do some shopping. I've nothing to wear, except what I brought in my flight bag."

"Oh, that's not a problem, we can all go shopping in the morning," Nikki said, obviously enthusiastic about the prospect of a shopping trip. "On the way here from the airport Eduardo pointed out some shops. I know just the place to visit. There's a shop on the Champs-Elysées that Eduardo has promised to take me to. Didn't you, Eduardo?"

Eduardo only nodded as he looked adoringly at Nikki.

Marc snapped his coffee cup back into place on its saucer. "I'm afraid shopping in the city is out of the question. Kate and I have to leave early. There won't be time," he said decisively.

"But surely it wouldn't take long for me to find something to wear," Kate protested. "I really do need some clothes for Cannes."

"Don't worry," he said. "We'll find you something. I'll phone through and order management to have the hotel's boutique opened early in the morning and made available for your exclusive use. Meet me in the lobby at seven sharp and you can have carte blanche. You'll be able to choose whatever you needed for the trip from our stock."

And Kate had to be satisfied with Marc's decision.

It was getting late and they were nearing the end of the meal when the maître d' brought the tab for the meal to the table for Marc to sign. Nikki and Eduardo, seeing that the evening was almost over, suggested all four of them should go out to a nightclub somewhere.

"As I said, Kate and I have an early start in the morning. Apart from traveling to Cannes, we also have some business papers we need to look over before our meeting with the Anistons."

Marc had put his foot down, but Kate felt a pang of sympathy for the two young people who had come to Paris with high expectations of having a good time. If she was in their shoes, she supposed that she too would feel disappointment at not being able to have a night on the town. Their frustration was clear to see on their faces.

"You're sounding like an old fuddy-duddy," Kate warned Marc cautiously. "They're young, and they want to enjoy themselves while they're here in Paris. Surely you can't object to them spending a few hours dancing."

"And you? Do you want to enjoy yourself at a nightclub?" he asked.

"We're not talking about me."

"Allow me to take the ladies to *Nuit Bijou*, Uncle Marc. I'll have them back at a reasonable hour."

"One moment, Eduardo. I was asking Kate a question." Turning to Kate, Marc said, "I'd like to know if you want to go dancing this evening."

She shrugged her shoulders and laughed. "I never go dancing, and I never go to nightclubs."

"What...never?" he asked, a look of surprise on his face.

Kate was amazed Marc would even think she was the type of person who had the time or the energy to spend hours on a dance floor.

"I'm always up early to start baking or preparing food for my customers," she explained.

Calling a waiter over, Marc said something in French that Kate was unable to understand. A few minutes later, before she realized what was happening and before she had time to protest, their party was ushered from the restaurant and steered outside to a waiting limo.

"Where are we going?" she wanted to know.

"I've decided that since you have no customers to please tomorrow, for once you can take the night off."

"Oh, you've decided, have you?" She was amused by his assertiveness, yet she was also put out by his dictatorial manner. Who did Marc Castell think he was and what made him think he could make decisions for her without taking her wishes into account?

"Yes," he said, placing a hand in the middle of her back as he firmly maneuvered her toward the door of the car. "Someone has to see you have a social life."

"And I suppose the person to do that is you?"

"For the moment it would seem so. Didn't Pansy or Paula, or whatever your assistant's name is, tell you to have a night out, perhaps followed by breakfast at Tiffany's?"

"What? Were you listening in on my conversation?"

Kate stood at the door of the car while Nikki and Eduardo clambered inside. She waited for Marc to answer.

"I didn't have much choice in the matter, did I? I was sitting right next to you on the plane."

"And her name is Patty, not Pansy, and it's extremely unlikely that I'll be having breakfast at Tiffany's, isn't it?"

There was a wide smile on Marc's face as he gave Kate a wink, and as he gently edged her into the limousine he said, "You never know."

Once seated, Kate suddenly thought she might need a coat or a covering if they were venturing out into the night. Although the day had been warm the evening was turning cool.

"Do I have time to collect a wrap from my room?" she asked.

"We haven't far to go, and you shouldn't need one," Marc said, and he was right.

Before Kate knew what was happening all four of them were on their way, traveling through the brightly lit Paris streets to spend the remainder of the evening at a nightclub.

As the limousine pulled into the curb Kate saw they were stopping outside an elegantly fronted façade of a classical Parisian town house. It was the *Nuit Bijou* nightclub. Doormen were in attendance, making sure everyone who entered were either on the guest list or were known to them.

The Castell party had no problem entering. They were immediately ushered in and shown to a secluded booth to the side of the oval dance floor. Drinks were ordered, but before they arrived, Nikki and Eduardo had already disappeared and had made their way onto the dance floor, leaving Marc and Kate seated alone at the booth.

Without the prying ears of Nikki and Eduardo, Kate had the opportunity to tackle Marc about the supposed catering contract he was offering her.

"I hope you realize I can't go into business with you, Marc. We decided that once this weekend's over we'd go our separate ways. That was the agreement."

Before they'd left the restaurant Marc had said something about looking over business papers in the morning. It seemed he hadn't given up on the idea of her joining his hotel-catering negotiations. But she wasn't backing down. She'd meant what she said about wanting nothing to do with the Castell men once this weekend was over.

"No, it wasn't," he said, lifting his glass. "That was *your* agreement. If I remember correctly, I said I'd try to persuade you otherwise. I wasn't the one who said we'd go our separate ways."

"Surely you can't expect me to continue as if nothing's happened. Not after we..."

"What? Not after we spend the night together?"

"Exactly."

Marc took a hefty sip of his whisky and returned the glass to its coaster. "Enough," he said decisively. "We haven't spent the weekend together yet and already you're worried about possibilities that might not even occur. Come on. It's time for us to relax and unwind. Let's follow those two...and dance."

"I'm fine, really. I don't need to relax, and I definitely don't want to dance."

The thought of having to dance with Marc had set Kate into a spin. Dancing with him would mean she'd have to be near him, close to him, touching him. No, she definitely didn't want to dance.

"You might not want to," he told her as he pulled her from the seat and led her onto the dance floor. "But I do...and believe it or not I need you to act as my partner. You wouldn't want me to look foolish dancing alone, would you?"

Marc smiled seductively and pulled her close, wrapping his arms around her. She didn't have a chance to reply. She couldn't. Enveloped in his arms, with her face pressed against the lapel of his evening jacket, her words would have been lost as they swayed to the beat of the music.

Somewhere in the crowded room Nikki and Eduardo were also dancing but Kate had completely forgotten about them.

With Marc's fingers curved around her waist, pressing into the smooth, silkiness of her blouse, and with her thighs pressed firmly against his, she could feel his sensual body as they moved to the rhythm of the slow, easy love ballad. The muscular hardness of his body was brushing against her frame and she knew she was arousing him.

It was only as Marc lowered his head and began nuzzling at the side of her neck that alarm bells started to ring. Kate's heart was pounding, beating overtime, and she knew she had to remain calm and composed. She couldn't let him see how much he was affecting her.

"I think this must be our song," he whispered in her ear.

It was a song she liked, but now it would always remind her of Marc and this moment. It would be Marc's song.

"Please, Marc...stop. We can't."

"Can't what?"

"We shouldn't be doing this."

"Why not? What's wrong with spending the evening together?"

"We ought to be leaving. We have to be up early," she told him.

"True, but that doesn't mean we can't have a night on the town. After all, we are in Paris—the city of the night, and the city of love."

"We really should be in bed."

"I know," he said softly, and on a laugh he asked, "Is that an offer?"

She didn't have time to answer. His lips found hers and any protests she might have made were silenced.

For the remainder of the evening Marc behaved. He was the perfect, attentive host, and it was with some reluctance when Kate, having caught sight of the time on Marc's watch, insisted they all made their way back to The Castell Plaza. It was two in the morning and she told him that if she was to keep to her agreement and be ready to travel tomorrow, she needed to get some sleep.

Soon after the two men escorted Kate and Nikki back to the hotel, and when they got there they all rode up together in the lift to the door of the penthouse. Kate was still amazed Marc had given up his private suite to her and Nikki for the duration of their stay. He could have given them one of the many luxury rooms in the hotel, but he hadn't. Perhaps he had an ulterior motive for having her sleep in his suite, but tonight she was too tired to think what it could be. She just wanted her bed...or rather his bed.

Promising to meet Marc that morning in the lobby, and having said her goodbyes to Nikki—

because no doubt Nikki would still be sleeping when they left—Kate went through into the luxurious bedroom and got ready for bed.

Undressing, her thoughts drifted back to the events of the day, and what a day it had been. That morning when she'd called at the beautiful Georgian house in Grosvenor Square she hadn't anticipated she would be whisked off to Paris—the city of love—in a private Lear jet or kissed by a seductive stranger. The day had been quite eventful, and it seemed there was to be an even more spectacular weekend ahead.

Tomorrow Cannes and Marc were on the agenda, but for now she was in Marc's private suite, lying between his silk sheets and sleeping in his king-sized bed.

Before Kate drifted off to sleep with the sounds of Paris floating in through the open window she briefly wondered what his next move might be but decided it was something she would have to tackle in the morning. She would face the problem of what to do about Cannes and Marc tomorrow.

For now she was content to pull the quilt over her shoulders, snuggle down into the luxury of his soft, feather pillows, and dream.

CHAPTER SIX

From beneath the warm bedcovers Kate reached out an arm and turned off the ringing alarm. It was seven in the morning, which meant she'd only had five short hours of sleep.

Yesterday when Kate mentioned to Marc that she needed to buy some extra clothes for her stay with the Anistons, she'd hoped to venture into the city with Nikki to get them, but Marc had swept all her wishes aside. And now she had to climb out of bed and meet him downstairs.

Even though she was fresh from sleep Kate felt fragile. Yesterday evening during the meal she hadn't drunk that much, but after a long emotional day, followed by an even longer night dancing the night away, everything had taken its toll on her.

The fierce, defiant Kate of yesterday was hidden somewhere behind her sensitive eyes, and by the time she'd showered and dressed in a pair of faded jeans and a fresh blouse Marc was already in the lobby waiting for her.

Like her, he too was casually dressed. He was wearing a pair of jeans and a dark blue shirt which matched the color of his eyes.

"Hi. How did you sleep?" he asked.

"Soundly, but short," she replied, and she had. Who wouldn't be able to sleep in such a luxurious bed as Marc's? Her only discomfort had been the blast of the alarm as it woke her from her dreams.

Marc looked at his watch. "We really should get moving. We're due to take off at nine, and by the time you've had breakfast and we've got to the airport we'll be cutting it close."

"Oh, I can skip breakfast. I'm not much of an eater anyway."

"You might not be, but I am. Come on. Let's get cracking and see what the dress store has to offer."

Marc moved off, and Kate reluctantly followed behind him until they reached the boutique shop a short distance away. He held the door for her, and as she walked inside she could practically smell the money hanging on the hangers.

This was no ordinary off-the-peg shop. Here designer labels were displayed by the dozens, and by the look of some of the clothes she knew they would be beyond her price range.

"I can't, Marc," was all she said.

"Can't what?"

There were several assistants in the shop and one of them was fast approaching. Kate tugged at Marc's sleeve, trying to pull him away, back out of the shop, but he wasn't moving.

"There's no point in me looking. They're not the type of clothes I usually wear," she told him hopelessly. "We'll have to go somewhere else."

"You haven't looked at any of them yet, so how do you know if you'd wear them or not?"

"Oh, I know."

The assistant arrived and Kate didn't have the chance to say any more as she was led over to the display racks.

"What exactly are we looking for?" the assistant asked.

"We'll take a look at everything," Marc said.

Walking around the store, Kate saw a cocktail dress she quite liked the look of, and reluctantly, as if she was touching something hot and forbidden, she took the dress off the display rack and measured the size of the dress against herself. She wanted to see if it would fit her figure. Everything in the store seemed to be a size zero. As she twirled and turned the dress in front of Marc he gave the dress a thumbs-down.

"Not your style and not your color," he told her.

There was no mistaking the fact that Marc knew what he was talking about. He was flicking through the designer dresses with such a studied expertise that it was obvious he'd done this many times before. Kate wondered how many different women had experienced what she was now experiencing with Marc.

"Try this on," he ordered as he removed a dress from the rack.

Reluctant to take the dress from him, Kate held back. "I think the other dress is a better fit," she told him crossly. "And it's more my style."

Marc was taking control and Kate was digging her heels in. She wasn't going to allow him to dictate to her, and she wouldn't let him tell her what she could or could not wear.

"Trust me," he said, as he took the dress she'd chosen out of her hands and replaced it with the one of his choosing. "This one is totally you, and it will suit your figure much better."

Marc was assessing her, and she could feel his eyes moving up and down her body; and he wasn't hiding the fact that he liked what was on view.

Kate could feel the heat of his desire hitting her like lightning, and the touch of his searching eyes as he ran them over her burning skin was electrifying. To avoid his stare, she darted into the small changing cubical at the back of the shop where she was out of sight and away from Marc's probing gaze.

Speedily, she stripped out of the clothes she was wearing, and when she tried his cocktail dress on, irritatingly and annoyingly, Marc was proven to be right. His was the better dress.

Knowing Marc would want to see what the dress looked like when she was wearing it, Kate cautiously pulled back the curtain screen of the cubical. Marc was waiting patiently.

"Well, does it fit?" he asked.

"I can't wear this," she protested. "It's gorgeous, but I can't wear it. It's too..."

"Expensive?" he asked with raised eyebrows.

The dress wasn't exactly beyond her budget. Yes, it was costly, but she had sufficient funds in the bank and her business was doing well enough for her to be able to afford it. It was the fact that it was a designer dress that made her reluctant to wear it.

When she'd been trying the dress on she'd had a peek and seen a well-known designer label sewn into the silk lining. Normally she would never splash out on a dress like this unless it was for a special occasion. And in her book, a weekend parading on Marc's arm and sleeping in his bed didn't classify as a special occasion. Acting as his companion wasn't a good enough reason to splurge her hard-earned money on a frock. She had more important things to do with her money. Usually she invested it or plowed it straight back into her catering business.

"I would never choose any of this," she said, indicating all the elegant things displayed around them.

"Look, Kate...but for the fact I've asked you to accompany me to the negotiations with Aniston this weekend you wouldn't have to buy or wear an evening dress. You wouldn't need a dress if it were not for you playing the part of my girlfriend, so I think it's only fair my company foots the bill. You'll need more than one dress, and you'll also need other things."

Marc was being practical, and she knew that what she'd brought with her to Paris wouldn't be sufficient to cover their weekend in Cannes.

"So you think I'm an eyesore. Is that what it is? What's wrong with my clothes?"

"Nothing's wrong with your clothes. I didn't say there was. Don't be so sensitive. It's not like you."

"I'm not being sensitive. And you don't know me. You don't know what I'm like," she told him.

"What's wrong now?" he asked, a frown across his brow.

Hesitantly, she went on, "I can't accept this."

"You have no choice in the matter. You know that eventually you'll have to accept my terms."

Marc was clearly becoming impatient by her resistance to accept the lavish and expensive gifts he was offering. It seemed that she was the exception to the rule. Did all women just take from him?

"I still think I'd like to go into the city to see what I can find to wear," she muttered.

"We haven't got time," he said as he glanced down at his watch. "We have to leave for Cannes within the hour."

"Then I'll have to make do with what I've brought with me."

She was defiant, but her protests were to no avail. They went unheeded. Marc signaled to one of the many assistants who were now hovering nearby.

"See to it Miss McKenna has everything she will need for her stay in Cannes. From the skin out. Beachwear, shoes, handbags, hats, the works. And have it all sent on ahead to the jet."

Without giving Kate the chance for further arguments, Marc took charge, and marching her out of the boutique and into the restaurant next door, they sat and had breakfast. True to his word, within the hour they had boarded the jet and were heading to the South of France.

* * * *

The jet flew them into Mandelieu Airport. They were here in the glorious, sunny South of France and their purpose was to thrash out the pros and cons of a global business contract.

Climbing into the sleek, black limo that Jeff Aniston had sent to collect them from the airport, Kate thought that now-or-never was time to tackle

Marc about the true reason he'd brought her here. There was bound to be some hidden motive.

"Explain to me why I'm here with you this weekend?" She turned in her seat and looked directly at him. "Apart from the fact you've blackmailed me...why am I really here?"

"Well…" he said, with a wayward smile. "Tonight is supposed to be an opportunity for everyone linked to the Castell-Aniston deal to get to know one another informally. We're here to party and mingle socially before getting down to business negotiations tomorrow morning. But if I'm honest, the main reason you're here is to keep me company." There was something boyish behind the glint in his dark, teasing eyes.

"And what exactly are we supposed to be doing?" she persisted, determined to get an explanation.

Marc reached for her hand as she sat beside him and started playing with her fingers. He laced his between hers, and his unexpected touch sent delicious shock waves surging through her body.

"We can do anything you like," he said provocatively. "And I like the way you said *we*. It means you're already thinking of us as a team...and as a couple."

"Let me make this clear, *Mr. Castell*. We are not a team, and we are certainly not a couple."

He leaned dangerously close toward her, and she felt his breath brush against her ear as he whispered, "Well, we soon could be."

Shocked by his evocative words, she pulled her hand away. "I could never consider having anything to do with a man who would force a woman into a relationship and into his bed. We are not a team and certainly not a couple. You have me for one night and one night only. That was our deal."

"A lot can happen in one night. In one night I could make you mine...*all mine*," he murmured, and there was a hint of certainty in his voice as he said those words.

Kate was frightened because she knew that behind his words there was some truth. There was no denying that there was a distinct possibility he could make her his. Already she'd discovered he had a certain power over her. He only had to touch her to cause a reaction.

Not wanting Marc to see her trembling lips or her tears of angry frustration as she fought to keep them at bay, she turned her face away and looked unseeingly out of the window at the passing scenery.

Usually she was a strong person. She could fight her own battles. But today she was tired and emotionally on edge. For some reason she was feeling pressured, and she was now trapped in Marc's world.

Not sure if she'd made the right decision, Kate wondered if she ought to have left her sister to make her own mistakes. After all, Nikki would have to grow up some time. Why not now?

Was she making a pointless sacrifice to protect her sister from an innocent friendship? Was it going to be all for nothing?

But by now it was too late for regrets. She'd made a deal. She'd asked Marc to intervene and in return she'd agreed to his terms.

A deal was a deal, and the debt had to be paid. Kate was here to fulfill her part of the bargain.

* * * *

It was only a short journey in the air-conditioned vehicle to their destination, and all too soon they arrived at the Aniston's luxury villa which overlooked the ocean.

As Marc and Kate stepped out of the limo Jeff and Robyn Aniston were standing near the main entrance waiting to greet their guests with a warm welcome. The place screamed money.

Although Kate came from a good family background, she didn't move in social circles that consisted of billionaires or jet-setters.

Men like Marc and people like the Anistons didn't visit the sort of places she frequented. They simply weren't in her group of friends. Since meeting Marc, Kate had been pulled through a whirlwind of emotions and events, and she didn't know if that was a good thing or bad. She wondered if Marc's lifestyle was going to be too much for her.

"Good to see you again, Jeff." Marc smiled as he shook hands with his host.

Jeff Aniston was a jovial man in his late fifties. With graying hair and a sizeable waistline he wasn't exactly the person Kate had imagined him to be. On the other hand, neither was Robyn. She was completely different from her husband. She was petite and young. You could almost think she was a trophy wife. But as Robyn stood beside Jeff welcoming their guests, Kate caught sight of an adoring look exchanged between the two, and Kate knew it was a look of true love.

This was no fake marriage. This couple was truly in love with one another.

"Glad you two could make it after all," said Jeff cheerfully. "We had news of a delay. Nothing bad I hope?"

"Nothing we couldn't fix," Marc said.

Marc had placed a hand around Kate's waist and was pulling her into his side, showing the Anistons that they were together, and that they were a united front.

Jeff and Robyn's home was on a hill overlooking the ocean, and during the afternoon Marc and Kate were shown around the place and given the grand tour of where they would be staying.

The villa was nothing like Kate had imagined.

She'd thought Marc and herself might be sharing a bedroom somewhere in the villa, but she was wrong.

Having taken Marc and Kate outside into the garden, Jeff and Robyn steered them around the sides of a spacious swimming pool, walking them through a canopy of mimosa trees until they came to the secluded guest annex secreted away and hidden from view.

The annex was in the grounds of the villa, situated on the edge of a white, sandy shoreline. The spot was idyllic. It was so serene and tranquil. With the blue waters of the Mediterranean Sea stretching out before them, the waves lapping gently against the shore, Kate felt a pang of envy. Who wouldn't want to live in this idyllic spot?

Tucked away from the main body of the house, the annex was a separate, self-contained unit. It was close enough for Marc to be on hand for negotiations yet far enough away from the house to allow for privacy. Even though Jeff and Robyn's offer of a place to stay was welcome, the seclusion of the annex had its drawbacks. Kate didn't want to be alone with Marc. The more she was with other people the safer she thought she would be.

After their hosts had finished showing them where everything was, Jeff and Robyn went over to the door to leave.

"We'll leave you two to settle in," Jeff said. "Dinner's served at eight or there about. Casual dress. Nothing formal tonight."

Marc nodded. "Sounds great."

"And it would be nice if you both came over for drinks before the other guests arrive."

"Other guests?" Marc asked.

"Yes. We've asked Cade and Yolanda to join us."

"Fine," Marc said, then shrugged his shoulders.

Robyn gave Kate a friendly smile before saying, "Kate, when Marc rang through last night to apologize for the delay he told us you'd made a last-minute decision to come away with him. If you should find there's anything you need, or anything you're short of, don't hesitate to holler. He also told us that you bullied him into bringing you here. Good on you, girl. Let *them* know whose boss, that's what I say. I always insist Jeff takes me away with him on business trips. He doesn't always like it, but it's something he puts up with because I would make his life a misery if he didn't. Wouldn't I, darling?"

"*Yes, dear*," Jeff said in a dry, humorless voice while rolling his eyes upward, making it obvious who wore the trousers in that relationship. Yet the loving smile and the wink he then gave Robyn told a different story.

"But I'm amazed you've done what you did, Kate. I don't think I'd have the nerve to tell Marc what to do," said Robyn. "I'm in awe."

"What I did?" Kate asked, surprised, wondering what Robyn could mean.

"Yes, he said you refused to stay in Paris and that you threatened to call off the engagement if he didn't bring you."

"*The engagement*?" Kate looked at Marc sharply. She was stunned.

"Yes, my love...*our* engagement," he said.

What was he talking about? And then she twigged. It was all part of the deception.

Kate didn't know if she should go along with Marc's blatant lie. Lying was against all her principles, and what he was asking her to do was to tell an untruth.

They simply weren't engaged.

What gave Marc the right to assume she'd play along with his new game of true love? But somehow, even though she wanted to correct his statement, the words of denial never came. She didn't know why she didn't tell Robyn and Jeff there was no engagement, but she didn't. Perhaps it was the way Marc was looking at her. It was almost as if he was challenging her to say it was untrue.

Well, if that was how he wanted to play it, Kate decided she would show him who was in charge.

"I know exactly how you feel," Robyn said sympathetically. "I feel the same whenever Jeff travels away on business and leaves me behind."

"Kate's a bit clingy at the moment, but I'm not complaining," Marc said, and from his great height he smiled affectionately down at Kate. Putting an arm around her waist, he planted a long, hard, possessive kiss on her surprised lips.

Robyn and Jeff were to be left in no doubt about Marc and Kate's relationship.

"Where's the ring?" Robyn asked as she looked at Kate's bare fingers.

"We haven't done a press release yet," Marc explained. "Kate's worried. She believes that if the paparazzi see us together and spots the ring, all hell will break loose."

"And she's absolutely right," Jeff said, sympathizing with Kate's supposed feelings. "That's exactly what happened to us. Wasn't it, darling?"

"Yes," Robyn said, and nodded in total agreement. "Life isn't easy when you're about to marry a super-hunk like these two. I hope you know what you're letting yourself in for, Kate. Having said that, I'd be happy to go through it all again. It's worth it just to be with Jeff and to be his wife."

Kate envied the Anistons' obvious love and closeness.

"Gosh, Robyn! Are you trying to scare Kate off before I've put a ring on her finger?" asked Marc on a laugh.

"I wish you all the luck in the world, Kate. I really do," said Robyn on a more serious note. "I know it's not going to be easy for you to accept women chasing after Marc, even after he's married. But I know you can do it. If you love him, they won't matter."

"Oh, I don't mind if they chase him. As long as he doesn't touch, I'll be happy."

Kate was getting used to her new role, and daringly, she planted what looked like a loving kiss on Marc's cheek. She wasn't sure how he'd take her comments, and she wondered if she sounded too possessive, but when everyone burst into laughter she was relieved no one thought she'd overstepped a boundary.

Having gone along with the pretense of an engagement Kate realized there was no turning back. At least not for now. What happened after she and Marc left Cannes...well, that was another matter. She would have to wait and see how Marc solved his problem of a non-existent fiancée.

"We'll be planning our wedding soon, and when we do, we'll be sure to let you know the time and place. We'd love to have you both at our wedding. Wouldn't we, darling?" Marc said.

The way he was looking at her she had no other option but to nod and agree. Kate could almost believe Marc meant what he was saying. She could almost believe they were engaged and that she belonged with him…and to him.

When Jeff and Robyn returned to the villa, leaving Marc and Kate to settle in, the annex suddenly became quiet. At a loss for something to do Kate began exploring the place and discovered she and Marc had use of a good-sized lounge, an adequate kitchenette, and two light and airy bedrooms. She assumed guests staying with the Anistons had use of these rooms and were only expected to join their host for meals. Under normal circumstances she would be extremely happy to stay here, but these weren't normal circumstances. She was here, and she was here sharing with Marc.

When Marc saw her moving toward the spare room he stopped her in her tracks.

"Don't you dare," he warned her. "Don't even think about it."

"Why not? No one will know we aren't sharing a room or sleeping together in the same bed."

"The housekeeping staff will know, and then everyone in Cannes will know. Cannes is a small world and here everyone knows everyone's business."

"What's wrong with us sleeping apart?"

"If we want to create the illusion of being in love *and engaged,* we have to act the part."

"Not *we...you.* It's you who wants to create the illusion."

"If I'm not mistaken, in Paris you promised to share my bed."

"But that was before I knew Nikki would be all right."

"But it was still a promise. Are you going to keep your word?" he asked.

"Of course."

She'd been backed into a corner and knew she was fighting a losing battle. Marc had found her weak spot, and she realized he wasn't going to relinquish any emotional hold he had on her. He'd discovered she was a woman who kept her word, and it was obvious he was using that weakness to his advantage.

"Look, we need to get along," he said. "We have to get used to being with one another. Outside there's a pool that looks inviting, and after being cooped up in the plane I should imagine a bit of exercise will do us good. How about a dip before we change for dinner?"

"Sure," she said, grudgingly going along with his idea.

Perhaps if they were outside in the cool of the afternoon and not in the hot confines of the annex she wouldn't feel so alone with him.

Reluctantly, she went through into the larger of the two bedrooms. It was the bedroom she would be sharing with Marc that night, and the large double bed against the window was the bed they would be sleeping in...together.

While they'd been on a tour of the house and grounds with Jeff and Robyn, their luggage had been brought to the annex and it was now standing at the foot of the bed. Kate started to unpack. Somewhere among all the new clothes she hoped to find something she could wear at the pool.

The shop assistant at the boutique had been told Kate was to have everything she could possibly need...from the skin out...and having followed Marc's instructions to the letter there was literally everything a woman could need packed into her cases.

Having hung most of her things in the closet or placed them into a drawer Kate was still searching for the elusive bathing costume when she came across what looked to be a couple of pieces of material connected by a drawstring. Surely this couldn't be the costume she was looking for! But it was...and she decided it was something she couldn't possibly wear.

Holding up the tiny scraps of blue material, she saw it was a bikini and it would barely cover the full, rounded curves of her breasts and hips. Nothing would be hidden, and nothing would be left to the imagination.

Going back into the lounge, Kate confronted Marc with the offending object. Holding the scanty bikini between her thumb and forefinger, she waved the offensive article, attracting his attention.

"That looks fine to me," he said, somewhat distracted. He was busy setting up his laptop on a desk in a corner of the room. "Go and put it on, and we'll take a dip."

"If you think I'm going to put this on and parade around naked for your benefit, you can think again," she told him, waving the flimsy scraps of material in the air.

Marc walked over to Kate, and taking the offensive bikini from her outstretched hand, he measured the material against her body. She felt his touch as his fingers accidentally brushed against her, and she moved hastily backward, out of his reach.

"It ought to fit. What's the problem?" he asked.

"The problem is...there's nothing to wear."

"Don't be a prude, Kate. No one's here to see you."

"You're here," she told him, and she reached for the bikini, snatching it out of his hand.

Flouncing away, she returned to the bedroom in a tiff where, unwillingly, and with no other option, except for two other bikinis which were in the exact same style only in different colors, she began to undress.

Dressing in a matching kaftan and slipping into a pair of sandals, once again Kate returned to the lounge to confront Marc who was still wearing his jeans and shirt.

Kate felt vulnerable. Standing beside him, she felt underdressed and practically naked. She was definitely out of her comfort zone.

"Satisfied?" she asked him, tilting her chin upward in defiance.

"More than." His sultry, admiring glance expressed more than his words could convey. "Give me two seconds and I'll be with you. If you'd like to wait while I change..."

"No, it's all right. I'll go on ahead," she said politely. The thought of him stripping in the next room was more than she could bear.

Kate only stopped long enough to collect the sunglasses she'd left on the table and snatch her tote bag off the chair before she rushed past him. Flinging the door to the annex open and making a speedy exit outside, she headed straight for the pool, hoping not to encounter anyone on the way. The temperature outside was intense, and as she neared the patio area where the pool was situated she could see the heat bouncing off the water. Removing her kaftan and leaving it with her bag on one of the loungers, she walked over to the pool's edge and dipped her toes into the refreshing, cool water.

A noise behind Kate caught her attention, and turning her head, she saw Marc approaching.

"Don't stop," he said. He was looking her up and down, and she felt uncomfortable as he admired what was on view. "I like a striptease. Especially when it's for my eyes only."

"In your dreams," she said, placing her hands squarely on her hips.

Dressed in black trunks, which showed off his tan to perfection, Marc looked handsome, fit, and athletic. He was pleasing to the eye and there wasn't a spare ounce of flesh on his lean, hard body. As he moved, the muscles on his abdomen rippled and she could tell he was in peak physical condition.

Slightly embarrassed at seeing his near-naked body Kate didn't wait for an invitation to enter the water. Instead, she plunged headfirst into the pool and disappeared from view.

She was a strong swimmer, and as her arms slashed out, cutting through the water, powering her back and forth across the pool, she felt as if the eyes of a dark devil were following her. And they were. Marc was watching her every move.

After several energetic laps Kate reached the side of the pool only to be confronted by Marc himself. He stood towering above her.

"Not bad," he said.

His compliment went unheeded. She was too busy pulling herself up out of the water. Breathless from her brief burst of activity, and with her energy waning, she tried with what little power she had left to extricate herself from the water.

She was struggling, and seeing her fruitless efforts, Marc reached down a hand, and with the ease of a practiced athlete, he plucked her out of the pool as if she was weightless.

"Thanks," she said, still gasping for air. "But I could have managed."

"I'll throw you back in if you prefer," he offered. He was still holding her against him and made a move to do just that.

"No...don't you dare," she squealed, caught off guard.

It was the worst thing she could have said, because as she squirmed and wriggled against him they both lost their balance and went tumbling headlong into the pool with an almighty splash.

Surfacing, Kate came up spluttering and giggling in amusement at the unexpectedness of what had happened. Marc had looked positively ungainly as he nose-dived out of control into the pool with her in tow.

Breaking the surface of the water, Marc dragged in a breath of air. "Wow...my side hurts. What was it you hit me with?"

She wondered what she'd hit as they fell and now she knew.

"It must have been my elbow," she confessed.

"Well, your elbow can sure give a man a dig in all the wrong places."

"Then you shouldn't have touched or threatened me in the first place," she told him. "It serves you right for messing about."

Daringly, Kate started thrashing her arms about playfully in the water as she tried to splash Marc in retaliation for what had just happened. Unfortunately, she wasn't having much success. Every time she reached for him, he darted with great skill and expert ease out of reach.

"Come on, Kate. You can do better than that," he teased. He'd obviously recovered from the blow he'd sustained, because he was circling her like a shark with great proficiency while gently flicking water at her with a foot or a hand in provocation as he swam past.

His taunting egged her on.

"Why did you push me in?" she called out laughingly as he edged his way to the side of the pool. "You are such a brute, Marc Castell. You wait 'til I catch you. I'll get my own back."

"Why wait? You can come over here and get your own back now. Or better still, I'll come and get you."

With lightning speed Marc plowed his way through the water and captured her in his arms. She struggled to remain on the surface and frantically paddled with her feet to keep afloat.

"You bully," she shouted, pushing hard against his broad chest as she squirmed in his arms, trying to escape. "Let me go this instant."

Her struggles were achieving nothing. Marc simply tightened his grasp, holding her firmly against him.

Gradually, he maneuvered them to a shallower part of the pool, but Kate's feet were still unable to touch the bottom. She had to cling to him for support. Their wet bodies were molded together and she couldn't break free.

"At last I've got you. I've been waiting all day to have you to myself, and now you're all mine and we can do whatever we like."

"No, we can't," she protested. "And I'm not yours."

She felt his hands reach for the fastening of her bikini top.

"No," she pleaded, but he didn't listen. The ties which held the tiny pieces of fabric in place were released. Her lips parted in surprise and that was all that was needed for Marc to make his move.

Slowly, his lips met hers, and then he plundered, taking what he wanted to take. Any protests Kate made were silenced with his kisses. Her head was being forced back and he was devouring her. With her neck arched and exposed she felt Marc nibble his way to her earlobe.

"You want me," he whispered against her ear. "I know you do."

They had reached the shallower end and were able to stand in the water but that was her downfall. Now Marc didn't have to support her and keep her afloat. His hands were free to explore her body more thoroughly.

She felt the intense sexual attraction between them surfacing. It couldn't be stopped, and she had to reach for him, touch him, and feel him. Raking her fingers into his hair and wrapping her arms around his neck, she gently gripped, holding onto his shoulders as she pressed herself against him.

His mouth descended and his tongue swept over her exposed, hardened nipples. He was stirring all kinds of emotions deep inside. There was a roughness as his tongue moved over the erotic zones of her body, and she couldn't stop him as he tugged at her brief bikini bottoms, loosening them so he was able to slip his hand inside.

His exploring fingers found a triangle of soft, delicate hair. Then, spreading his fingers through the silkiness, he worked a finger deep inside her. He was teasing and pleasuring her with his touch and she was ready for him, but more importantly she wanted him. Opening her legs and wrapping them around his waist, she pressed herself against his swollen rod.

All day the tension between them had been building . Every touch, every gesture, every look had been leading up to this moment. Things were spiraling out of control, and she was on the point of coming. She wanted him to take her and make her his, and she wanted him now.

"Steady, Kate," he told her calmly. "We've got all weekend to explore each other's bodies. There's no rush."

Breathlessly, she let out a moan.

"Marc..." She sighed, wanting more than he was giving.

"Why hurry?" he asked. "Take it easy. We'll get there."

She was falling for him in a big way. She was seeing another side to the ruthless, powerful, dynamic businessman. She was seeing a softer side of Marc she hadn't known existed. Here was a kind, considerate lover, and he was going to teach her things about her body she never knew.

* * * *

Marc was determined to get to know Kate, not just in a physical way, emotionally as well. He wanted to know the real Kate. He wanted to know what made her tick. What were her passions? What was vital to her wellbeing?

Physically he knew there would be no problems between them. He'd sensed from the very beginning they were meant to be together. No woman had ever affected him the way Kate did. She only had to be in the same room as him and he was aware of her, felt her presence, and wanted her. And she responded. Kate reacted to him in a way he had never known before. There was an instant, intense chemistry between them that had to be satisfied...and it had to be satisfied soon.

Then from out of the corner of his eye Marc saw a couple emerging along the path from behind the concealing shrubbery. They were fast approaching the pool area and were bound to spot Kate as she clung to him, practically naked.

Seeing the floating bikini top which was within reach, Marc made a grab for it and passed it to Kate.

"Here...put this back on, quickly," he whispered urgently in her ear. "Follow what I do and say."

"What?" Kate asked, surprised.

"I said...follow my lead."

Without warning he kissed Kate hard and passionately, which caused her to splutter and sink. The two of them were still entangled and she was taking him down with her to the bottom of the pool.

When they surfaced, gasping for air, they were still locked in a tight embrace.

"Hello...What's going on here?" someone asked.

The couple continued to approach the pool and as they did so the man gave a wave to Marc. The newcomers were stylishly dressed and looked as if they would be staying for dinner.

"Hi, Marc."

"Cade...I didn't know you'd be here so soon. I thought you were joining the Anistons for dinner. But now that you're here...how are things?"

Marc was doing his best to shield Kate from prying eyes as she hastily put the bikini top back on. He was also acting as if he'd only just become aware of his friend's appearance.

"Robyn told us you were coming to the house for dinner, but Yolanda couldn't wait. We were on our way over to the annex to see you," Cade explained. "We heard the noise and wondered what all the commotion was about. It looks like you two are having fun."

"Yes, we are," said Marc as he pulled Kate close. "Now that you're here, why don't you and Yolanda get changed and join us?"

The woman was playing with her hair and tweaking a ruffle on her dress. "Not now, darling. You wouldn't want me to ruin my hair, would you? Can't you see I'm dressed for dinner?"

"And you look very nice," Marc complimented.

Yolanda was wearing a sophisticated haute couture gown and shoes that were anything but the casual dress code Robyn had mentioned. Jewels dangled from her ears, a string of diamonds circled her neck, and her fingers were encased in sparkling gems.

In the pool Marc was steering Kate tactfully to the ladder where he helped her to climb out. As their bodies emerged, dripping and spraying water everywhere, Yolanda looked questioningly at Marc and slightly disdainfully toward Kate.

Reaching for a bath towel which was lying on a lounger, Marc quickly covered Kate's exposed body from the disapproving stare.

Rubbing and drying Kate with the towel, he was unconsciously touching and feeling her body in such a way that the onlookers were left in no doubt he and Kate were on intimate terms with one another. And although the act of drying the moisture from her body wasn't done in an erotic way, his delicate, tender caresses couldn't have been more explicitly sensual.

"It's obvious you two aren't going to be ready for dinner on time." Yolanda sounded bored and affronted.

"We'll be with you as soon as we've dressed. It shouldn't take us more than fifteen minutes to get showered and changed, but if we're delayed it will be all Kate's fault. We arrived from Paris and she immediately wanted to unwind and *play* for a bit." To the others it was obvious what he meant by the word *play*. The play he had in mind wouldn't be an innocent game of tiddlywinks. Their game would be hot, steamy, and sensual.

Everyone at the poolside was imagining an energetic romp between the sheets, and Marc could see the shy blush of embarrassment begin to spread across Kate's cheeks.

"Aren't you going to introduce me to your...*friend*?" Yolanda asked while firing a look of contempt in Kate's direction.

"Yes, of course," Marc said coolly, ignoring the raised eyebrows and disdainful glance. "Yolanda, Cade...may I introduce Kate McKenna...*my fiancée*."

CHAPTER SEVEN

The word *fiancée* had hardly registered before Marc was once again kissing Kate passionately on the lips. It was a deep, devouring kiss that made Kate's head spin and sent her world turning upside down.

He had said she was his fiancée.

"Kate, this is Cade Knightley and his...umm, lovely wife, Yolanda," Marc introduced. "You've heard me mention the Knightleys before."

So this stunningly attractive woman was Yolanda. The woman Marc was trying to avoid. The woman he wanted to build a barrier against. But Kate found it difficult to believe Marc needed her there to keep Yolanda at bay. Surely he didn't need anyone or anything to shield him...especially against a woman. Kate wondered if he was using her as a smoke screen to pull the wool over Cade's eyes.

There was still time to throw a spanner in the works. She could still blow Marc's plan to smithereens. All she had to do was deny the engagement. If she was going to let the cat out of the bag, now was the time for her to deny any relationship with Marc, before things went too far. She could say he'd brought her there under duress. That she wasn't his loving, adoring fiancée. That she'd never met him until yesterday...but she didn't. She stayed silent.

Kate sensed that the almighty Marc Castell was indeed vulnerable. She could smell trouble in the air and could see by the look in Yolanda's eyes that something sinister was brewing. Marc was walking on eggshells.

Kate hadn't yet worked out what was going on between Marc and Yolanda, but she knew something was wrong. Perhaps Cade was ignorant of an on-going affair between Marc and his wife, or perhaps in a subtle way Marc was telling Yolanda that their relationship was over. Kate didn't know what was happening between the three of them, and she didn't really care. It wasn't her problem...only it had become her problem, because Marc was involving her in his personal life.

Kate shivered, and even the hot heat of the afternoon was not enough to stop the goose-bumps from appearing. She could guess at the lengths Marc would go to in order to achieve his goal, and she also realized there would be nothing she could do about it.

If Marc wanted her to play a loving *fiancée*, then that was exactly what she had to do in order to get through this weekend, and keep Nikki safe.

Reaching for her kaftan which was on the lounger, Kate put it on. Marc also picked up the cargo shorts he'd discarded earlier and pulled them on over his wet trunks.

Throwing a towel over his shoulder and an arm around her waist, Marc looked at Cade and said, "We'll see you both over at the main house for cocktails in about twenty minutes if that's all right with you."

"Sure, sounds good to me," Cade said.

"We'll try not to keep you waiting, but it will depend on how long Kate takes to shower and dress."

"I'd say longer than twenty minutes," Yolanda said cattily. "I expect it will take Kate at least an hour to put on her makeup."

The comment was a backhander and Kate knew it.

"Oh, if we're late I doubt it will be because of the time Kate needs to get ready for the party. It will more than likely be because of the time we'll need in the shower. You see, I like to have my back washed and..." There was no need for him to say any more. Yolanda got the message.

Doing an about-face, Yolanda walked off toward the house, leaving Cade to follow. Kate and Marc gathered the remainder of their belongings and strolled the short distance back to the annex.

However, all was not calm. Once inside the privacy of the annex Kate turned to Marc and confronted him with her anger.

"So, this is the reason you've brought me here," she said bitingly.

"Just a second. What reason are you talking about?" he asked, running a hand through his dark, damp hair. He squared his shoulders as if preparing himself for her onslaught.

"Yolanda," she said. "Surely you don't seriously believe I can keep Yolanda away from you. Because let me tell you...I can't."

"Really?"

"Yes, really. I saw the way she looks at you. And if a woman like Yolanda wants a man, she'll get him. Nothing I do or say will stop her."

"Oh, I think you could deter her if you tried. And if you put your mind to it, I expect you could deter any other woman I might know."

"You mean there are more like her?"

"What do you think?" he teased. Laughter was dancing in his eyes.

Kate couldn't take it any longer. She had to get away from him. She'd blow her top if she continued to listen to his provoking remarks.

Turning her back on him, she walked across the room and into the kitchen. Opening the fridge, she retrieved a carton of orange juice and was about to pour a drink when she noticed Marc had followed her. It seemed their discussion wasn't finished.

Frustrated, she slammed the door shut, and pouring a glass of juice, she offered it to Marc, but he refused. Instead, he opened the fridge and took out a can of lager.

Pulling the ring on the can, he took a large gulp before saying, "Where were we? Ah...yes, Yolanda."

"I think if Yolanda wasn't married you two would be ideal for one another."

"But she is married, and she's deadly. You know she is. Kate, you've seen what she's like. I need protection from her. She's lethal."

"Yes...lethal to the wallet."

The picture of Yolanda in her haute couture gown and jewels surfaced in Kate's mind.

"That's the problem exactly...and she wants me."

"You can handle her. I know you can," she guffawed with mock concern.

Kate couldn't take Marc seriously. A man of his ability, a mega-tycoon, a person with his amount of self-assurance could surely handle anyone. But it seemed not.

"Usually I can deal with her type, but I don't want to have anything to do with a woman who's married to my accountant. I don't mix business with pleasure. It tends to get messy."

"Ah, you mean you would have an affair with Yolanda but only if she wasn't married to Cade."

"I didn't say that. And who's to say I haven't already had an affair with her?"

"Have you?" Kate asked fiercely, and then wished she hadn't. She hoped Marc didn't think she cared one way or another who he'd slept with.

"It's none of your business who I've bedded," he told her brutally. "My past is just that...the past."

Kate noticed he hadn't answered the question. She knew he was no saint. It was obvious that he'd had affairs before. Affairs that had possibly included married women, but it seemed he had some scruples about cheating on a friend.

"I saw the way you two were looking at each other," Kate said. "And it's clear to me something's going on. I'm only surprised Cade hasn't picked up on your vibes. Or perhaps he has."

Kate was standing with her hands on her hips, waiting for Marc to deny her accusations. He didn't. Or at least what he did say wasn't exactly an outright denial.

"My friendship with Cade is important to me. I've known him since university, and from the moment he introduced me to Yolanda...well, she's been off limits. You might not know this, but it's sort of an unspoken rule between gentlemen. We never touch one another's women. And you're mistaken," he said. "There's nothing of importance between

Yolanda and myself, and there never will be." He sounded like he was joking. With his usual caustic sense of humor he was dismissing her concerns, tossing them aside as if they were of no importance. Then he said, "On the other hand, there could be something very serious between you and I."

"A serious relationship with you?" Kate snorted. "Thanks, but no thanks."

Kate refused to believe Marc was serious when he said there could be something between them, and she certainly wasn't going to become involved with him only to be counted as one of the many women who passed through his life. She deserved more from the man in her life.

"You know I can make you want me, Kate," he told her, and she was amazed at his self-confidence and conceit.

She tossed back her head, squared her shoulders, and looked defiantly in his direction. "You can try to make me want you," she said, braving his wrath. "But you won't succeed."

"You know you're wrong...and this evening I intend to prove it." There was a hidden challenge and a flash of excitement in his eyes as he said those words.

She could tell Marc was planning something, he was plotting, and whatever it was she was determined she wasn't going to give in to him.

"Sure," she said. Her gaze was fixed unwaveringly on his. "You might be able to arouse me physically but—"

"There's no *might* about it. You know I can arouse you."

"But you'll never have me. You'll never have my heart, my mind, and my soul."

The dare was all Marc needed to spur him on. He carefully placed the can of lager he was holding on the counter and took her untouched glass from her hand, setting it next to his drink.

Leisurely and with deliberate precision, he trailed a long, slender finger across her bare shoulder. His caressing touch was cool as he ran it back and forth provocatively along her exposed collar bone. Then, tracing the outline of her bikini and toying with her shoulder strap, he moved his fingers across her skin, working his way down toward the valley between her breasts.

Kate stood frozen. The unexpectedness of his caressing attack sent her reeling. As she felt his touch she took a weak intake of breath. Mesmerized, she couldn't breathe as delicious shivers of excitement were coursing their way through her body.

He was thrilling her senses. She could smell the freshness of him. His body scent was awakening her desires, filling her senses with awareness. Marc was right...he did indeed have the power to instantly arouse her.

Her skin was on fire, her heart rate was soaring, and blood was racing in her veins. From somewhere deep inside an intense burning heat was spreading to her inner core. Dressed only in her flimsy kaftan she could feel the hotness radiating from him as their bodies touched.

"We have to get ready for dinner," she protested weakly, trying to find a reason to break away from him.

She pushed at the solid wall of his muscular chest but it was no use. He wouldn't let go. His fingers continued to caress her, to touch places that were throbbing with need, and there was no stopping him.

"I'm not hungry for food," he murmured. Capturing her face in his hands, he bent his head, whispering in her ear. "I'm only hungry for this..." His lips nipped gently at her earlobe. "And this…" he said, trailing soft kisses down to the base at her neck. "And this."

Tenderly, he rained light, butterfly kisses across her face until he reached her throbbing lips. As much as she twisted her head and arched her neck, trying to avoid his seeking lips, she couldn't evade his mouth as he plundered and captured hers.

"Marc, we can't do this," she whimpered.

Did he know what an effect he was having on her? Was he intentionally playing with her emotions and driving her wild with his kisses, only to prove his point? She knew only too well that he could arouse her. But did he have to do it with such skill that she melted at his touch?

"We can't do what?" he asked. He'd slipped a hand beneath her kaftan and removed it from her shoulders, allowing it to fall unnoticed to the floor.

Kate couldn't help her response. Against her will she was trembling with desire in his arms. As she looked up at him through veiled eyes, she could see the hungry need in his gaze. The way he was looking at her, with unfathomable longing and a deep craving, had her head spinning. She was weak at the knees and holding on to him for support. She tried to think clearly, but it was no use...she couldn't.

Marc curved an arm around her waist and pulled her close, into him. Her heartbeat raced as she felt his hard desire pressing unyieldingly against her. There was no mistaking the fact that she was arousing him.

The solid hardness of him throbbing against her made her more than aware of his urgent need, and there was nothing she could do to stop him. The erotic, sensual feelings surging through her as their bodies touched was matching his. They were both on fire and they needed fulfillment.

Dressed only in their swimwear they were practically naked in one another's arms and the hot, burning feel of his skin next to hers had her wanting more. Of their own accord her arms reached up and wrapped around his neck. Threading her fingers through his hair, she matched him kiss for kiss as his searching mouth probed.

Marc wasn't holding back. His hands traveled upward from her waist until they reached her breasts, and through the material of her bikini she felt her nipples harden. They were taut, rigid, straining, and they wanted to be released. All it would take would be one small tug at the tie string that was holding them in place and they would be freed. But Marc didn't pull.

As one of Marc's hands cupped and played with her nipple his other hand reached down toward the fabric of her bikini briefs. One of his muscular legs eased between hers. He'd spread her, holding her open to his touch as he slipped his fingers beneath the fabric.

Kate was wet and ready for him. Teasingly, he explored the soft curls of silky hair surrounding her center, and as he parted her folds and hooked a finger into her core she could feel the juices oozing from her.

A tremor of longing surged through her. The rough feel of his finger and thumb as he played with her clitoris had her panting with need, and she was dizzy with yearning.

Resting her head against his chest, she tried to regain her balance. She wasn't sure if she was holding on for support or because she wanted to get nearer, but whatever the reason it didn't matter, because at that moment he stopped and gently pushed her away.

Kate couldn't fathom it. Why was Marc exciting her, bringing her to a point of no return, only to reject her? What was he doing? Was he being cruel to be kind?

"We haven't time," he groaned with frustration.

Kate felt a cold rush of air come between them and a sense of loss came over her.

"When we make love I want to make love to you slowly," he told her. "I want time to savor and taste the moment. I want to pleasure you and bring you to your climax. Kate, I don't want to take you only to satisfy my sexual appetite. When we make love I want you to have as much satisfaction from being with me as I intend to have by being with you."

Hearing his words, she felt relief. Marc wasn't rejecting her. He'd had his reasons for calling a halt to their lovemaking.

She'd been given a reprieve...yet in another way she felt she'd been deprived of something, but she wasn't sure of what.

Throughout the day, the feel of Marc's hands on her as he accidentally touched her or brushed against her had been having a desired effect. He'd been driving her crazy with longing; and knowing that at some point during the weekend he was planning to make love to her was acting as a kind of long, drawn-out foreplay. She hadn't expected her feelings to be so intense or so extreme when she was with him, but they were.

Marc hadn't been playing with her. He'd been exciting her. Making her ready for what was to come. Gradually, he'd brought her to a fever pitch of desire, but now that he'd withdrawn, she couldn't help but feel bereft.

"Get dressed, Kate," he ordered. "You're far too tempting dressed as you are, and if you don't go now, we won't be having dinner this evening."

The threat of what he intended to do if she didn't dress galvanized her into action. Retrieving the discarded kaftan from the floor, she covered herself before fleeing to the bedroom where she showered and changed for dinner.

* * * *

Arriving at the main house, Marc and Kate were ushered through the grand hallway entrance into an even grander lounge.

Glancing around, Kate noticed that the room was nearly full. She estimated there were about thirty couples present, and by the nods and smiles Marc was receiving it looked as if some of the people were already known to him.

The large floor-to-ceiling French windows leading onto the patio were open, allowing a cool, refreshing evening breeze to drift in and flutter the finely spun curtains with its gentle gusts. Drinks and canapés were being served by waiters who went from guest to guest with silver trays balanced dexterously in their hands. The buzz of conversation filled the air along with the background music from the stereo system. And with strategically placed lighting bouncing off the glittering jewels of the guests and gleaming crystal drinking glasses, the place sparkled like a palace.

Tall, broad-shouldered, and dangerously handsome, Marc stood out in the crowd. He was a man to be reckoned with. Dressed in a dark suit with a crisp, white shirt and a silk cravat tied loose at the neck, Marc's groomed and sexy presence was unmistakable. His deep tan gave him a Mediterranean look, but if anyone heard his accent they were left in no doubt he was French.

Acutely aware of him at her side, Kate's senses were heightened by his nearness. With his possessive hand pressed into the small of her back she was intensely aware of his touch, and against her will she couldn't help the rush of excitement that ran through her because of his closeness.

Tingling charges were coursing through her body, and he had her melting. But that wasn't the problem. Kate's problem was the constant flashing images crossing her brain, reminding her that a short time ago they'd been locked together in one another's arms, practically naked.

It seemed strange to be dressed and behaving politely in a civilized manner to one another, when earlier they'd been entangled in a hot, steamy embrace that had nearly led to the bedroom.

When Marc moved, brushing her with a hand or an arm, it only increased her awareness of him, and if he intended to tease and torment her with his light, intentional caresses, she knew she wasn't going to make it through the evening.

Kate didn't know if his actions were deliberate or not, but either way there was no avoiding his constant contact. As a waiter passed with a drinks tray Marc handed her a martini and their fingers briefly brushed. When their eyes met, she froze.

"Drink it," he told her. "It will steady your nerves."

There was nothing wrong with her nerves. True, she was shaking inside, but that had nothing to do with nerves. It was Marc that was making her tremble.

"But I don't like martinis. I'd much rather have a juice or something."

"Drink," he ordered, and by the way he was looking at her she knew it would be best if she took at least a small sip.

When she tried the drink she was pleasantly surprised. It tasted quite nice. It was refreshing, cool, and not too dry, but as she wasn't used to drinking alcohol, a short while later, when a waiter was passing, she replaced the glass on a tray. Marc raised a brow questioningly but offered no comment.

The evening had well and truly begun.

* * * *

Marc's arm was wrapped firmly around Kate's waist, holding her close and pulling her snuggly against his side; it seemed the right place for her to be. Together they looked like the ideal couple.

Tonight Kate was wearing the black lace cocktail designer dress he'd chosen for her that morning, and there was a polished elegance about her that made her instantly noticeable.

Viewed from the front she was demurely covered from head to toe in the fine, lace webbing, and the dress fluttered sensually against her legs when she moved. But when she turned, the open back of the dress plunged downward toward her waist, revealing the long, slender curve of her spine and her smooth, naked back.

With her hair piled high on her head she looked tall, sophisticated, and graceful.

Marc recognized that Kate had inborn breeding and class, and tonight it was apparent.

Tonight it was on display for all to see. She was his woman, and he wanted everyone to know who Kate belonged to.

Stunningly beautiful, she had a quiet charm and an understated loveliness that shined from her sparkling eyes. She stood out in the crowd, and envious glances from both the men and women were drawn to her in admiration.

Women always flocked to Marc, hoping to attract his attention. They wanted to win his approval and arouse his sexual curiosity, but tonight he wasn't looking. His interest was only for Kate.

Although Marc had originally asked Kate to accompany him to Cannes to act as a buffer, he now realized he wanted more from her. He wanted Kate to be his totally and completely. In the fullest sense of the word Marc desired her, and he wanted her...body and soul. Normally a man of supreme confidence, he was unsure if she would even consider a serious relationship with him.

As the evening progressed and dinner was over, everyone moved into the drawing room to relax and unwind over coffee and liqueurs. But instead of joining the group, Marc and Kate migrated out onto the terrace to sit in the cool of the night. He steered her along a path until they reached a bench under a vine-covered pergola where they could sit. It was a secluded spot away from the noise of the other guests and away from the safety of the party.

"How's your weekend been so far?" he asked. Leaning back, he stretched out an arm, resting it along the back of the bench and around her shoulders. Touching her seemed natural. It felt so right.

"Thinking about it, I suppose I ought to say my weekend's been quite sensational." Kate looked at him and smiled. "It isn't every day I get to fly in a private jet to Paris or I'm taken to the South of France for business negotiations. And it's not every day the Castells of this world come into my orbit. But do you want to know what I really think of my weekend so far?"

"Yes, I'd like to know."

"Well, if I'm truthful, I'm glad I found Nikki and she's safe. I also have to say I've enjoyed meeting the Anistons. They're wonderful people. And Robyn...I have so much respect for her. She's built her own interior designer business up from scratch, and it appears she's doing really well."

"Yes, the Anistons are great when you get to know them. And as for Robyn...the two of you have much in common."

"How can you say that? I'm nothing like Robyn. Look at what she has."

Marc held Kate's chin between his fingers and turned her to face him. "What does she have that you don't? Robyn has intelligence, and so do you. She has a thriving business, and so do you. And she has a man at her side...and here I am. Need I say more?" His voice was intense, and he meant what he said.

Kate laughed light-heartedly, and she flushed slightly, clearly embarrassed by his compliments. "So far this weekend's been amazing," she said. "But if you were to ask me would I prefer to be here or working in London, I'd have to confess work would win. I have the future to think of. I also have a living to earn."

"Your skill in that department will be tested tomorrow during negotiations. I know you don't believe me, but I'm serious when I say I'd like to offer you the catering contract. Castell Hotels and Aniston Travel will need a good caterer."

Marc was thinking of using McKenna Catering to provide a catering service for the Castell Hotel Group after he'd noticed a certain niche in the market. Many of the guests staying in his hotels or traveling with Jeff's company were foreign tourists visiting London to see the sights. They often booked one of the coach daytrip excursions that left the city early in the morning and returned late at night. These visitors frequently made a request, asking if it was possible for the hotel chefs to provide them with a packed lunch of some sort, but unfortunately, due to the fact that the chefs were either serving breakfast to the guests or they were preparing food for the hotel's evening menu, it wasn't always possible to accommodate their needs.

That was when Marc came up with the idea of providing outside catering...and that was where McKenna Catering came in. If Kate could provide a pre-ordered packed meal Castell and Aniston would be able to generate another source of income. Kate didn't know it, but Marc had big plans for McKenna Catering. Once the operation was up and running in London, his intention was to expand their resources to cover the United Kingdom before going global.

All that needed to be done was some number crunching concerning the budget...and more importantly, for him to persuade Kate that McKenna Catering was a necessary element in the grand scheme of things.

"There's bound to be a catch," she said. "Your offer sounds too good to be true. Tell me, Marc...what would I have to do to win the contract?"

Without knowing it Kate had fallen into his trap. She was showing an interest, which meant she might be open to his business offer.

"If I was the type of person to take advantage of a situation, I'd suggest sleeping with the boss might help. Like...right now."

Marc pulled Kate to her feet, pressing close against her. Looking down, he saw a fevered hunger burning in her eyes that equaled his. There was an urgency, a desire and a longing pulsing in the air between them, and the throbbing sexual tension was electrifying.

"I think it's bedtime," he said seductively.

Hungry for a kiss, he looked with yearning at her moist, red lips, but before he could pull Kate into his arms, Cade and Yolanda came out of the darkness of the night, walking toward them.

"So here you two are," Cade said, not realizing what he'd interrupted. "We wondered if you'd already left the party."

"We were about to leave. Kate told me she wants an early night." Marc's arm was now placed possessively around Kate.

"Sounds like a good idea." Cade grinned. "Perhaps Yolanda and I ought to head for our hotel as well."

Yolanda looked coquettishly at her husband then turned toward Marc.

"Marc, darling...after the meeting tomorrow Cade and I are planning a short trip along the coast, and we thought you might like to join us for the afternoon. It would be great if you came."

Marc gave Kate a quick, surreptitious glance that spoke volumes, and she got his message without him having to say the words…*I told you so*.

"That would have been nice," he answered, going easy on the sarcasm. "But I'm afraid we've already made plans. After the meeting I'm taking Kate to buy our rings."

A look of shock and disappointment coupled with a look of frustration was apparent on Yolanda's face. But it was nothing compared to the surprise on Kate's.

"Couldn't you go shopping another day?" Yolanda persisted.

"Afraid not," Marc said bluntly. "Tomorrow we have a big day ahead of us. So if you two will excuse us...I think it's time Kate and I called it a night."

With his hand placed on the small of Kate's back, he gently, but with firm determination, began steering her in the direction of the annex.

CHAPTER EIGHT

Arriving at the annex, they entered and once inside, closing the door behind them, they shut out the world and the sounds of the night. In the silence of the room, even with Marc there, Kate felt alone and isolated. And the sexual tension between them was mounting.

Slipping off his jacket, Marc tossed it carelessly onto a nearby chair, and loosening his tie, he went through into the bedroom.

Without bothering to switch on a light Kate was compelled to follow him until she came to a halt, standing in the bedroom doorway. Frozen to the spot, she stood looking with dread at the large king-sized bed before her. It was the bed they would be sharing together. The bed in which they would be spending the night.

It occurred to her that someone had visited the annex while they had been at the house. The covers on the bed were turned back and it looked like the room had been especially prepared for them.

"You'll have to come to bed sometime," Marc warned her.

Kate wasn't moving. She didn't want to enter and was still standing near the door. She felt it was her last chance to make a dash for freedom, but her legs weren't moving.

"Are you sure I have to share that bed with you?" she asked anxiously.

"I'm sure."

"But no one would know if we didn't sleep together," she persisted.

"The servants will know," he said as he gestured toward the bed that was so invitingly prepared for them.

With the light of the full moon shining into the room Kate could see a scattering of soft, scented rose petals across the white satin sheets. It was obvious someone had thought romance was in the air.

Her reluctance must have been evident because Marc walked forward until he stood facing her, and then he wrapped his arms gently around her, cradling her body against his. She sensed he was giving her time, reassuring her, telling her there was no rush, but they both knew what was going to happen.

There was no need to pretend there wasn't a sexual attraction between them, because there was. It was tangible and they both felt it.

Marc was having an effect on her and by the way her body was pulsating and trembling at his nearness they didn't have to say they wanted each other...they both knew.

All evening they'd been working toward this moment, and having been constantly in one another's company the tension and sexual attraction between them had been growing. Finally they were alone, and what was about to happen was inevitable. The moment was here.

Kate's mind was in turmoil. She knew she was attracted to Marc physically. There was no denying the way her body reacted to his slightest touch, but she was unsure if she could commit to this man emotionally.

Could she love a man who had brought her to Cannes solely for his own purpose and pleasure? Could she be in love with someone who was domineering and egotistical, not to mention self-opinionated? She doubted it. Yet there she was with a man who disregarded her wishes to achieve his own desires. And then she realized that the answer to her inner doubts was simple...she didn't want to be in love with him, but she believed she was. At that precise moment Kate knew she had fallen for him, and she had fallen hard...and she wanted to run.

Marc carefully tilted her head up toward his. Raining light kisses along her jawline, he searched until his lips found hers; then slowly parting her mouth with his tongue, he teasingly probed.

Delicious shivers ran through Kate as he began working his magic. With wanton passion she returned his hungry kisses, and shamelessly she wanted more. Her arms, as if with a will of their own, were reaching up, clasping him around his neck, and she pulled him closer.

"Marc," she moaned with longing as she felt the rough stubble on his chin rasp against her cheek. She needed him, and she needed him now. In that instant Kate made a decision, and it hadn't been an easy decision to make. She decided she was going to give herself to Marc...tonight. She wasn't going to resist his advances. She would be a willing partner in their lovemaking, and she would be giving as much as she hoped to receive.

Never before had she felt so attuned to a person. From the moment they'd first met she knew he could affect her like no other man could. He only had to look at her to make her tremble. And when he touched her, she melted.

Without hesitation, Marc lifted her into his strong, muscular arms and carried her across the room toward the bed. Reaching for the bedside lamp, he was about to switch the light on when she stopped him.

"Please, Marc." And there was no need for her to say more.

In the darkened shadows of the room, Marc slowly slipped the dress away from her shoulders. He eased the material down, and her bare skin was exposed to his penetrating gaze. It was a sensual torture.

The silky, lace dress fell from her body, gliding and pooling onto the floor at her feet. Shortly thereafter her skimpy underwear followed. Kate was standing before Marc...naked.

She felt vulnerable and insecure, but not for long. Daringly, she undid one button on his shirt, then a second one. When she heard his sharp intake of breath, excitement coursed through her veins. It was obvious her touch was arousing him and she knew she had a certain power over him.

With a simple stroke of her fingers against his bare skin she discovered she could make him react to her touch. She was sending him wild and she was stirring his blood.

Reaching for the fastening on his trousers, Kate opened the zipper. Slipping her hand inside the waistband, she found him hard and ready for her.

He was solid, heavy and stiff. His foreskin was stretched, engorged with blood, and his rod was pulsating with a desperate need. Stroking his long, hot tool in her hand, she closed her fingers around his shaft and squeezed gently. Marc groaned his satisfaction.

"Don't stop," he murmured, breathing heavily.

Kate could feel his sticky pre-come on her fingers and knew he was nearly ready for her. His manhood was swelling, increasing further in size, and the blue veins along his shaft were pulsing and throbbing as they filled with blood.

Hurriedly, he pushed her back onto the bed before quickly removing the remainder of his clothes. Carelessly, he discarded them, dropping them unnoticed onto the floor before joining her on top of the smooth, silk sheets covering the bed.

The cool of the evening breeze came wafting through the open window, washing over them, and in the light of the moon they looked at one another's bodies, naked and exposed.

Running his fingers back and forth from her breasts to her thighs, Marc had her writhing and panting hungrily beneath him. As he cupped her breasts in his strong, masculine hands, she fit perfectly. It was as if her body had been made for him.

He rubbed her hardened nipples provocatively between his thumbs and fingers. Lowering his head, he took one into his mouth. Rolling his tongue around the engorged peak, he nipped and sucked while his other hand slowly glided downward.

A ripple of pure, sensual pleasure flowed through her as his fingers reached the small triangle of fine hair covering her sex. But Marc wasn't lingering. Little by little his fingers slithered further down until they arrived at the soft, delicate flesh of her inner thighs.

"Steady, Kate...steady," he whispered reassuringly as his fingers drew near to the source of the incessant throbbing between her thighs. "There's no rush. We have all night."

"Don't stop," she whispered, and as she held on to him she gasped, struggling for breath. "Please...don't stop."

Uncontrollably, she thrashed her head from side to side on the pillows as she fought the raging passion building deep within. There was an ache, a pulsating yearning of such intensity between her legs that she thought she would faint with desire. Urgently, she lifted her hips from the bed and began grinding against Marc, longing to get closer.

Marc forced a leg between hers. He was pinning her down, holding her open to his touch as he explored, stroking her sensitive zones until she was whimpering with pleasure beneath him…and she wanted more of him.

Her arms were spread-eagled and her legs spread wide. She was vulnerable. Helplessly, she lay there waiting for his attack. She wanted him to take her, possess her, and do with her as he wished. But Marc wasn't giving her what she needed.

Unable to stand the delicious torture and dizzying heights to which he was carrying her, she was compelled to beg for more. She wanted instant release. She needed to be filled and taken to a point of climax, but he was taking his time and was in no hurry to reach his goal.

Unable to bear his exquisite torment any longer, Kate clenched her fists into tight balls and clutched desperately at the bedding beneath her. She was experiencing sheer torturous delight as she pressed herself against him, wanting him to take her then and there.

Her gaze locked with his, and she couldn't look away. She felt his hands exploring, seeking the tangle of soft, curly hair between her thighs, and then at last his fingers were exploring further, delving into a hot, secret place that was waiting for him.

It was the place she'd kept hidden from anyone's touch. It was a place that until now only Marc had found.

* * * *

Marc wanted to savor every moment he had with Kate. He wanted to delay her final release of sexual satisfaction, and the longer he could do that, the better.

Parting the moist folds of Kate's lower lips, he uncovered her throbbing clitoris. With probing fingers, he found her opening. He was at the entrance to her wet core, and carefully, he inserted first one finger and then another. She was tight, but gradually he eased her open.

Pulling back and forth, he moved in and out until her sticky juices began seeping and oozing from her onto his fingers. With his fingers still inside, he used his thumb to rub roughly against her clitoris, bringing her to the brink of orgasm.

"Marc," she moaned frenziedly. "Please, Marc."

But he wasn't listening to her cries of desperation, and although he was on the point of coming, he held back and moved away from her. He knew she wasn't ready for their final joining. Even though she was wet enough and open enough for him to enter her, he needed Kate to want him with every fiber of her being, the same way he wanted her.

He knew she wanted sexual satisfaction, but he wanted her to connect with him emotionally, merge with her mind and with her heart, and not just with her body. He was going to make her wait until she was ready to give him what he needed. But their time to join together as one wasn't now. The moment wasn't right. When they finally made love, as he knew they would, it had to be perfect. He wanted her to be sure she knew what she was doing. Making love had to be Kate's choice. She had to make the choice with her heart, not with her libido, and especially not because he'd asked her to spend the weekend with him.

Tonight was about Kate. He needed to pleasure her and know that their lovemaking would be as mind-blowing an experience for her as it was going to be for him. And there were to be no regrets.

"We're going to take it slow. I want to know you. The real you. I want to know what pleases you, Kate. I need to know what you like and what excites you."

"I'm ready," she pleaded. "Please, Marc...please."

He silenced her cries with a kiss, then concentrating on her swollen clitoris, he made small, circular movements, twirling and rubbing her hardened nub between his fingers and thumb. Kate bucked, lifting her pelvis off the bed toward him, but he moved over her, pressing her down into the mattress. Keeping her in place and within reach of his skillful fingers, he worked his magic.

Then stepping up the pace, he had her squirming with delight as he began vigorously rubbing her clitoris. Kate was rocking back and forth as he moved his fingers from side to side across the soft inner lining of her womanhood. The friction was sending her wild. Her slender thighs were clamping down hard on his hand, and she was holding him deep inside her as she ground against him, searching for her release.

He was taking her over the edge and beyond the point of no return.

* * * *

Kate buried her face against Marc's shoulder as an uncontrollable orgasm shook her body, and unable to stop herself, she released a shriek of elation into the darkness of the room. He'd brought her to the summit of sexual bliss and taken her to heights she'd never imagined were possible.

When it was over, she lay in his arms gasping for breath, then turning away, and with her back to him, she curled herself into a protective ball. Wave after wave of wanton gratification continued to surge through her body, and she knew she had to be away from his touch, even if it was only briefly. His caresses were too painful, too pleasurable, too much for her to withstand as she tried to recoup from the satisfying experience she'd just endured.

Acutely aware of her nakedness and vulnerability, she clutched at the silk sheets, attempting to shield her body from his all-seeing eyes. Shock after shock of sensual, orgasmic ripples pulsed through her. He had carried her to heights she'd never known existed. He'd given her pleasures beyond her wildest dreams, and yet he hadn't taken her, not completely, not totally. Marc hadn't penetrated her with his manhood.

Cradled, spooned in Marc's arms, he was leaning over her hot, burning body, gazing at her face.

Kate slowly raised her arms to shield her eyes from his searching stare, but it was to no avail. Marc reached for the lamp on the bedside table, and switching it on, the room was bathed in a muted, warm glow.

Lying next to Marc and bathed in the afterglow of their lovemaking, Kate felt a deep sense of satisfaction. She was sure Marc could tell by the look on her face and rise and fall of her breasts as she let out long, contented sighs of fulfillment, that she was sated.

"Don't ever hide from me, Kate. Let me see you," he said, planting soft, tender kisses along her exposed back.

Turning her to face him, Marc was once again searching for her lips, and when he gave her an all-consuming kiss she had no option but to respond with equal passion.

"How was it for you?" he asked when her trembling and shaking had subsided.

She moaned shyly with pleasure against his chest. "You know how it was for me," she said.

Kate knew Marc hadn't come yet. He was still fiercely erect, and his hard, pulsing rod was engorged and demanding attention. Stretching her body sensually against him, she felt his hardness and knew he was ready and wanting her.

Marc had been concentrating on her needs and her desires, and now it was her turn to please him.

Reaching down, she took hold of him, and using both hands, she began caressing his stiff rod. Running her fingers over the oozing wet tip of his shaft, she had him jerking uncontrollably at her touch.

Her touch was sending Marc wild. His engorged rod was rearing its head, ramming hard against her. Rolling her over and taking control, he pressed her down into the soft pillows beneath them.

She shifted, willingly parting her legs in readiness for his assault, but it didn't come. Instead he only kissed her.

Marc was taking her to new heights and to new extremes of pleasure. He was exploring every inch of her enflamed body, leaving no place untouched or unseen, until once again she was on the point of exploding.

When he touched her womanly mons she couldn't resist, she reached down and held his hand there, pressing his fingers against her aching clitoris.

"Faster, Marc. Faster," she pleaded on a moan. "No...no...please...harder," she begged as her breasts rose and fell against the rough hairs of his bare, masculine chest.

Then the red-hot burning heat of desire spread through her once again as Marc dipped his fingers in and out of her wet core like a piston. She was ready for him, and she was coming, over and over.

Kate felt like she was being hit by a bolt of lightning as spasm after spasm shot through her, leaving her quivering with uncontrollable desire. Once more she was gushing and spilling her juices onto his teasing fingers as she climaxed.

But Marc held back. He still wasn't entering her, and he still hadn't come.

Exhausted, Kate lay in Marc's arms, and after a while he reached over and turned off the bedside lamp. Turning back the covers, he left the bed.

"Where are you going?" she asked, concerned. She wondered what she'd done to make him leave her so abruptly.

"Go to sleep, Kate," he whispered. Bending down, he planted a long, hard kiss on her mouth. "We have to be up early tomorrow. We've reports to read and figures to run through. I want you fresh and clear-headed in the morning. I want you to know what you're getting yourself into if you join forces with me this weekend."

There was a double meaning to his words...and she heard them.

Join forces. Marc wasn't speaking only about the business deal tomorrow. And she knew exactly what he meant.

"You don't want to make love to me?"

She was perplexed by the sudden turn of events. Her emotions were charged, and she needed him. She wanted to give herself to him, but it seemed Marc didn't want to make love. He was telling her to go to sleep.

"Make love to you? Of course I want to make love to you. It's about the only thing I am certain of at this moment," he said without any hesitation. "You're a very desirable woman. What man wouldn't want to spend the night with you?"

Spend the night. That didn't sound like a commitment. "But I want you to make love to me," she said pleadingly.

It was obvious Marc liked the fact she was expecting to be made love to and sexually fulfilled by him, but he hadn't made love to her. He was making her wait; denying her the pleasures she so desperately craved.

"What is it?" she asked, puzzled. "What have I done? I thought you wanted me and that's why you brought me to Cannes."

For some reason Marc's rejection hurt. She was offering herself to him and he was refusing that offer. And she didn't know why.

All day the tension between them had been building. She'd reached a point where she was charged and ready to give herself, but it seemed he was blowing hot and cold.

* * * *

Marc had never intended to force Kate into his bed for the purpose of making love to her. His original plan had been to create an illusion of being a couple. It was to fool the world and Yolanda into believing they were together. Never once had he said she *had* to have sex with him, and never once had he considered she would.

He knew she was disappointed that he hadn't made love to her. Of course he wanted to; there was no doubt about that. But he wanted more. He wanted a meaningful relationship and not just a brief fling. For a man who never went anywhere with the same woman twice, he was in grave danger of finding total commitment.

But despite the fact he hadn't actually made love to her, he knew he'd brought her satisfaction. That had been more than evident by her responses. Pride had filled him as he watched the emotions ripple across her face as she reached orgasm.

Gently, Marc caressed her cheek. "Kate, how can you think making love to you was *the only reason* I brought you to Cannes?"

He sensually stroked his fingers across her parted lips, then walked into the en-suite where he took a much-needed long, cold shower. Coming back into the bedroom, refreshed and sexually eased, he found her still awake. She was waiting for his return.

"Go to sleep, Kate. I need sleep even if you don't." Climbing into bed, he pulled her snuggly against his naked body, and cradling her into the warmth of his arms, they settled down for the night.

* * * *

Kate could feel the coarseness of the fine hairs on Marc's legs rasping against her thighs. Still sexually charged from their earlier encounter, the feel of him brushing against her skin was exciting. She longed to turn in his arms and begin their lovemaking over again, but she didn't. She wished she could switch off as Marc had done. She wanted to disconnect from the tension that was still buzzing between them, but she couldn't.

Spending the night sleeping next to him as if it were the most natural thing in the world was going to be torture. Yet with her emotions still in complete turmoil, it wasn't long before she heard the deep, even sound of Marc's breathing as he lay sleeping beside her.

How could he fall asleep when she still needed him? Sleep was the last thing on her mind. She never thought she would ever want a man this much...as much as she wanted Marc, right now…but she did.

Kate had always secretly thought she was frigid, but tonight Marc had proved her wrong. During the short time she'd known him he'd turned her world upside down, and now she knew what it meant to want someone. Kate wanted Marc, totally, desperately, and in the fullest sense of the word.

In the darkness of the night she lay listening to the steady rhythm of his breathing, and when she stirred, intending to move to her side of the bed to give him more room, his arm instinctively snaked out and tightened, holding her fast. Gradually, the tension eased from her limbs and then she too drifted off into a peaceful slumber, secure in the protection of his warm embrace.

* * * *

In the early hours of the morning either a noise or some disturbance outside must have woken them. Throwing back the covers, Marc told Kate to stay where she was, and leaving their bed, he went over to the bedroom window to investigate.

As he stood framed in the window Kate caught a glimpse of him silhouetted in the light of the moon. His naked body glistened in the shadows, and viewing him from where she lay, she thought he looked magnificent. The muscles on his lean, bronzed torso rippled as he moved, and in that moment she knew she wanted him like she had never wanted anything or anyone before.

"Whatever it was seems to have vanished," he said, and then he went back to bed and to Kate's open, welcoming arms.

Pulling him down onto the bed beside her, she pressed her body urgently against his, showing him her need.

"Are you sure?" he asked.

"Of course," she told him. She took the initiative and began kissing him heatedly.

"We shouldn't..." he said, making a valiant attempt to resist her.

But as they gazed into each other's eyes they both saw their matching needs and urgent desire. Marc stroked her hair back from her face, then hungrily sought and found her eager lips. She wasn't holding back.

"I know that now is the time for our next step," he whispered, and then there was no going back.

Raking her hands in his dark hair, she dug her fingers gently into his scalp. She pulled him down until his mouth swept over the peaks of her hard nipples. He was stirring all kinds of emotions deep inside her, and with a certain roughness, his tongue moved over the erotic zones of her body.

With each action he dragged her willingly along on a tide of erotic passion. She could feel his hands on her naked skin as he explored her body, and once more his hands traveled downward until he came to the triangle of soft, silky hair between her thighs.

Raking his fingers along the crevice of her opening, he worked his fingers deep inside. He was teasing her, pleasuring her, and she was wet and ready, and wanting him.

As Marc played with her throbbing clitoris, moisture oozed from her sex. And when he teased his thumb around and around the sensitive button of her core she felt the intense heat building to a crescendo as her inner muscles clenched and convulsed.

Sucking hard on the peaks of Kate's aching nipples, he pushed and plunged his fingers deep inside her. Kate squirmed as she was gripped in spasms of delight. Her hunger was building to such a fever pitch that she knew he had to fill her and take her. She needed to reach orgasm soon.

"Marc...I need you," she gasped pleadingly.

As she said those words Marc turned away from her, and for one fearful moment she thought she'd done something wrong. But Marc had only turned away so he could open the drawer of the bedside table and reach inside for a condom.

Turning back to Kate, and pressing his mouth to hers in a long, lingering kiss, he rolled the condom over his erect manhood. Parting her legs with some urgency, he was spreading her lower lips open, preparing her for his assault.

Kate clung to him, holding him tightly against her. As her hips bucked in a frantic frenzy beneath him, his heavy weight pressing down on top of her was exquisite. She needed to feel him deep inside her, and she needed to feel him *now*.

"Please," she murmured, pulling him urgently toward her.

With her legs wrapped tightly around him there were no barriers separating them, and there was nothing stopping him from taking her and doing with her as he wished.

Marc's rod was solid, hard, and hot. He was engorged and ready. He was positioned at her wet opening, and placing his shaft at the entrance to her core, he began pushing until gradually he gained access. Slowly, he entered her slippery, moist opening.

Her opening was tight, very tight, but he wasn't stopping. With the force of his weight behind him he was entering and spreading her wide. Kate gasped as his manhood filled her. He thrust until he was deep inside her, filling her completely, and then he lay still—immobilized. She assumed he was giving her time to adjust to the size and feel of him.

"Are you all right?" he asked with concern.

What Marc didn't know was that Kate was untouched; and under no circumstances did she want him to know he had taken what no man had been offered.

Kate was a realist. She knew she'd only been asked to Cannes as a decoy for his affair with Cade's wife. She also knew he treated women as a disposable commodity, but tonight that didn't matter. Tonight she wanted him and she was using him as much as he was using her.

Kate knew Marc could have his pick of any woman he wanted, and she also knew he wasn't going to offer her a lasting relationship. This was a weekend fling. Their affair wasn't serious. There was no future for them, but that was all right. Tonight she was with him, and that was enough. It would have to be.

From the first moment she'd seen Marc she knew the inevitable would happen, and it was happening...now. She was here. She was in his bed, and they were joined together as one. Marc Castell was deep inside her, and with his hard rod filling her completely, she was soaring to unbelievable heights and going to sensual places she'd never been to before.

"Are you all right?" he asked again.

"Marc…" she whispered, and released a groan of sheer pleasure, telling him all was well.

Instinctively, she rolled her hips, and grinding her pelvis against him, she clamped down hard upon his shaft with her inner muscles, causing him to groan.

Slowly, Marc began his beating rhythm. First he withdrew until he almost left her, and then he lunged back inside. Gradually, his forceful thrusts began pumping harder and faster. His tempo was building to a crescendo, and as he continued pounding his thick rod into her it became an unbearable sweet torture...but it was a torture she relished.

As his swollen rod was withdrawn and inserted it rasped against her sensitive clitoris, sending Kate into spasms of delight. The heavy weight of him as he lay on top was almost more than she could bear, and as he thrust deeper and deeper, filling her completely, she wanted to savor the exquisite moment of pain and pleasure forever.

Marc's breath fanned her face. His breathing was labored but she hardly noticed. They were too busy reveling in the sensual feel of one another's bodies as they slid into positions of torturous delight.

Sliding in and out, Marc pulled her closer, nearer, until there wasn't an inch of space between them. His engorged rod was ramming cruelly, almost brutally inside her, but she was relishing in his forcefulness.

"Harder...harder," she whispered against his ear.

And yet again he was bringing her toward another mind-blowing orgasm, only this time it wasn't his fingers working their magic, but his hot, blood-engorged shaft. He was deep inside, filling her, and she was swollen and bursting as his length and width consumed her. Kate surrendered completely to the moment.

Her inner muscles were clamping hard around his shaft, and as she tightened, squeezing down on him, she started milking him with her wet embrace. Instinctively, she knew what to do. She was a natural, and she soon discovered what excited Marc and what pleased him the most. But he was insatiable. He was taking more and more from her. And as he gripped and crushed her beneath him, there was nothing she wasn't willing to do.

Raking her hands into his hair, she clung to him savagely as they both reached the crest of their orgasms. Fused and joined together, they merged as one. Time was frozen as spasm after spasm surged through them.

Finally, as an all-consuming orgasm washed over her, Kate whimpered his name.

"Marc..." she gasped breathlessly with satisfaction.

In the aftermath of their passion, when their heartbeats had slowed and their yearnings had been sated, Marc began showering tender, soft kisses across her closed eyes.

His hand lovingly pressed her head against him, cradling it in the crook of his neck, and in the darkened room, with the frenzy of their lovemaking over, entwined in one another's arms, they fell into a deep, relaxing sleep.

CHAPTER NINE

Although he'd been awake for some time, Marc was still in bed. Lying on his side with an elbow resting on the pillow and his head propped on his hand, he was content to watch over Kate as she slept peacefully beside him.

The events of the night were still fresh in his mind, and it had ended better than he could have ever imagined. His weekend with Kate was turning out to be quite an experience. He hadn't expected to share such passion with her, and he hadn't expected she would be willing to give so much of herself to him, but she had. It was an encounter he wasn't likely to forget.

Their lovemaking had been unconditional. She'd given him pleasures that had set his heart racing, and even now he was on a high. Thinking about how she'd responded in his arms had him wanting to wake her and make love to her once again, but he resisted. He was in no hurry to move. For now it was enough just to be here beside her...and look.

* * * *

Kate began to stir and she woke slowly, stretching and yawning herself into the new day. The sunlight filtering through the fine lace curtains danced across her skin, and opening her eyes, she didn't know if it was the sound of Marc's voice or the feel of his lips against hers that was stirring her senses.

"Good morning," Marc murmured quietly. "How did you sleep?"

She was acutely aware of his presence beside her, and her heart pounded with excitement at his nearness. She had instant recall. Flashing before her mind's eye were images of all that had passed between them during the night, and a sense of awkwardness washed over her. She felt embarrassment for the way she'd behaved, for her naïve womanly wantonness, and for her insatiable appetite for Marc.

How could she have behaved like that? How could she have done the things she did and let him do the things he'd done? But most of all, how could she have responded in such a way...and enjoyed it?

Marc trailed a finger delicately across her jawline. "For someone who said she doesn't sleep with a guy on the first date—I'm honored. Do you know how much you amaze me? I hadn't realized there was so much passion in that petite, little body of yours."

She groaned and turned over, burying her face in the pillow.

"Tell me," he said as he placed a kiss on her bare shoulder. "Where have you been hiding, and why haven't we met before this weekend?"

Kate didn't believe in casual sex, and waking up in a strange bed, with a strange man, was something she didn't do. It wasn't in her character, and it certainly wasn't in her grand scheme of things. She was lying next to a man she hardly knew...and she was naked.

She'd never been prepared to have a *casual-temporary* relationship or a one-night stand with anyone. She was waiting for love and the right man to come along. And Marc couldn't be that man...could he? Not after knowing him for such a short length of time. Yet there she was sharing a bed with him. But thinking about last night, Kate thought that perhaps Marc might just be *Mr. Right*.

Never before had she felt so attuned to someone. Not only did he stir her physically, he also challenged her mentally. But even with the intense chemistry between them and their shared passion, she couldn't be falling in love with him...could she?

This man stood for everything she detested. His love life was shallow. He had a playboy lifestyle, and he discarded women like they were toys. From the moment they first met there had been an electrifying attraction between them. Sparks had flown, and last night she'd been unable to deny Marc what he had taken and what she had freely given.

Desire had flared, and it was a desire over which she'd had no control.

To her horror, Kate suspected her heart was no longer hers to command. Her worry was that against her better judgment she'd fallen totally, and without any reservations, in love.

"Uum...morning," she mumbled into the softness of her pillow.

Pulling gently on her shoulder, Marc turned her over so he could look at her face once again. His fingers began caressing along her jawline, and the pad of his thumb was pressing her lips open.

With his eyes still focused on her, he held her gaze, and she couldn't look away as his hands started moving over her body. Beneath the thin silkiness of the sheet the outline of her breasts could be seen, and when Marc cupped them in his hands her nipples became hard and taut...and then he moved lower.

"Shall we have breakfast?" he asked, planting light, lingering kisses along her neck.

His mouth was working its way toward her lips again, and she couldn't answer. She couldn't move. Against her will her blood was stirring and she was aching for him. A compelling pulsation was once again between her legs and an urgent need to have him *there* and touch her *there* kicked in. And it was a need that couldn't be ignored.

Lying beside him as he touched and caressed her most intimate parts, she became instantly ready and wet. She wanted Marc desperately, but it was a desperation she had to contain. He mustn't guess and she mustn't reveal to him how much she needed him.

"Breakfast?" she asked. She was thrown by the question. How could he think of breakfast at a time like this? Surely he didn't expect her to eat when all she could think of was the way he was touching her, feeling her, and caressing her. Her mind and body were craving other things, not food. "No...I don't need breakfast."

"And I think what I have here will fulfill my appetite," he said.

Marc pulled the sheet back, exposing her hard nipples. Lowering his head, he hungrily planted soft kisses around them before sucking the tight, pointed tips into his mouth.

The only thing on Kate's mind right now was making love to him over and over again. But she knew they shouldn't make love. She didn't dare risk it. It would be too dangerous. Their one night of lovemaking would have to last her a lifetime. If she let Marc make love to her a second time, if she let him touch her and take her once more, she knew it would destroy her. She would be his to own. His to have and possess. He would hold her heart totally, and she wouldn't have the will or the power to walk away.

After last night she knew her life would never be the same again. She was forever changed. Last night he had been gentle, caring, and giving. She'd felt cherished, and she would never forget their night of amazing tenderness and shared passion. But it wasn't love. Was it? Even though she might think she loved him, what they had shared couldn't be called love. Or could it?

"Are we getting dressed?" he asked in his deep, sensual French accent. "Or are we staying in bed?" There was a teasing invitation in his voice, but it was an invitation she couldn't accept.

Life would be too complicated if they made love again. She knew Marc's reputation. He was a *love them and leave them* type of guy. Life would be impossible knowing that any relationship they shared, no matter how brief, would eventually have to end.

No, it was best if she called a halt before they went any further. She couldn't let herself become emotionally involved...but perhaps she already was.

Kate's instinct was to walk away now before she got burnt by Marc's hot passion. He could make any woman feel special, and she did feel special, but she knew it was best if she remained independent and aloof from him.

Knowing Marc was a taker and not a giver, she decided she wasn't willing to wait around for any scraps of physical love he was willing to throw her way. If he wanted a woman in his bed to satisfy his needs, he would have to look elsewhere. She wasn't going to make herself available.

"I'm getting dressed," she told him. Galvanized into action, Kate threw back the bedding and slipped carefully from between the sheets.

"What's the rush?" he asked.

"If I remember correctly, you have a meeting. That's the reason we're here in Cannes, and that's the reason we have to rush. There's the Castell-Aniston deal you have to attend...remember?"

With nothing close to hand to cover herself with, Kate padded naked across the bedroom toward the en-suite. Marc's eyes followed her hungrily until she reached the door.

"I could put negotiations on hold," he shouted after her with a grin on his face. "But only if you make it worth my while."

"But it wouldn't be worth *my* while. Jeff would murder me. And anyway, I know how much he's counting on the deal going through, so you have to be there."

Kate went into the bathroom, closed the door behind her, and turned on the shower. She stepped under the hot, stinging spray and began soaping herself.

Yesterday evening during dinner she'd come to realize just how important joining resources with

Castell Hotels was for Jeff Aniston. Jeff revealed he was in trouble. Not financial trouble, but there were concerns that other competitive travel businesses were setting a precedence. They were taking the lead and offering a certain type of package deal to customers. It was a package deal that Jeff couldn't compete with alone. That was why Marc—as a friend—was stepping in and helping out. There was really no need for Marc to invest in Jeff's business, but he was going to do just that. And according to Jeff, Marc was acting above and beyond the call of friendship.

Although it was still a business deal, with all the cut and thrust of commerce, it was mainly a business deal between friends. Jeff couldn't sing Marc's praises high enough, and that was why Kate knew this morning's meeting was of vital importance.

"Jeff will survive, but I don't think I can." Marc had silently entered the en-suite and had joined her under the shower.

His soapy hands circled her body, and as he pulled her back against him, she felt the hard pressure of his erect penis pressing against her and a pulsing ache of longing began between her legs.

Kate needed no second bidding. Eagerly, she turned in his arms, and reaching up, she slid her hands behind his head and pulled him down toward her waiting lips. Their desire for one another was ignited.

Kate's intention of ending her relationship with Marc before it begun was gone. In that split second she accepted the fact that she going to give herself once more to Marc, even though she knew he was going to break her heart. It was simple, and there was no question about it—Marc was there, he wanted her, and she was longing to feel him deep inside once more.

Forcing a leg between her quivering thighs, Marc spread her open and gained access. He parted her moist folds and dipped his long fingers in and out, and as he did an anguished moan of desire escaped her lips.

She was nearing an orgasm, and Marc cupped his hands around her buttocks and lifted her high, positioning her above his stiff manhood. He was about to enter her, and in a frenzy of need she wrapped her legs tightly around him. She was wet and ready for him.

"Wait...condom," he groaned, but they both knew it was too late. They'd gone beyond the point of no return.

He was in place, and his rigid rod was seeking entry. With her wet slit open, he slowly lowered her until she slid gently down along his hard shaft.

Marc had impaled her onto his stiff erection until she could go no further. And with his tool buried deep inside, she'd been filled to the hilt—completely.

Marc held her against the shower wall and lunged into her with short, sharp thrusts as the hot spray from the shower beat down on them. Over and over, he continued pumping, battering against her slippery entrance, and all the time he was rubbing hard against her pulsating clit. He was bringing her to a fever pitch of excitement...and she wanted more. She couldn't get enough.

As he plunged, thrashing in and out, she clung to him in desperation. She was frantic for him to bring her to a point of climax, and she needed him to finish...soon.

"I need you," he said, and still deep inside, he forced her arms and legs wide apart and spread-eagled her against the hard tiles of the shower wall.

"Don't stop," she whispered against his lips.

Tomorrow they would face the consequences of their lovemaking...but not today. Fused together, merging as one, his seed exploded, spilling into her in hot, gushing bursts.

Kate froze in Marc's arms. She couldn't move. Her sticky juices were flowing in equal measure as his load was pumped and discharged into the deep valley between her thighs.

Their orgasms were cascading over and over, and clinging together for support, they melted in a release of sweet, satisfying pleasure.

* * * *

It was nearing ten o'clock before the committee assembled. Jeff had turned his library into an office for the day, and any persons of importance with any input in the matter were now gathering to thrash out the pros and cons of the travel deal.

Kate had read several of the reports in front of her, and so far the catering deal looked like an offer she couldn't refuse. She was tempted to commit herself and say yes, but something held her back. She needed to be sure. She needed to know it was the right thing to do. That it was right for her, and right for the workers she employed.

Sitting beside Marc at the conference table, she felt like part of the team. She was enjoying the cut and thrust of commerce as she followed the debates as they shared their ideas and visions for the future. She was also learning that Marc was prepared to do battle and could be quite ruthless when it came to the business of capital investment.

Toward mid-afternoon everyone broke for a late lunch. Leaving the library they'd been working in, and drifting outside into the cooling air, they began joining their families for a meal in the garden.

Most of the adults were milling around, circulating with pre-luncheon drinks in their hands. And those that weren't, were either sitting at the long wooden table on the terrace in the shade of the vine-covered pergola, protected from the overhead rays of the burning sun, or simply chilling. Slowly but surely everyone was recovering from the grueling conference they had just endured.

Across the patio children's laughter could be heard as they amused themselves near the pool, and somewhere in the distance the sound of music came wafting toward them on the breeze. It was an idyllic place to be. Everyone was relaxing, and for a brief hour they were getting away from the intense pace of the talks before returning to the hard task of battling out contracts and agreements.

Everything was fine, and everyone was getting along until Yolanda passed by with a glass of wine in her hand. Colliding and knocking against Marc, the contents of her glass spilled, drenching his shirt with a dark red stain.

Although the incident appeared to be an accident, Kate suspected otherwise. It seemed obvious to her that Yolanda had specifically targeted Marc to gain his attention. But what her motives were Kate couldn't be sure.

"Marc, how clumsy of me. Here...let me dry it," Yolanda said. Using a flimsy handkerchief, she dabbed at his shirt. It was a futile effort, and it only caused the deep, red stain of the wine to spread further.

The shirt had been ruined, and knowing it couldn't be worn during the afternoon's discussions, Marc had no alternative but to return to the annex and find a fresh one. Placing his drink on a table, he made his apologies.

"I think it best if I change," he said.

"I'll come with you, Marc," Kate offered. "It won't take—"

"No, stay where you are and finish your drink," he said. "I'll be fine. And when you see Robyn let her know she can start the meal without me. I shouldn't be too long."

Before Kate had a chance to protest Marc planted a brief kiss on her lips and made a quick exit from the terrace. Vanishing behind some shrubs he left a surprised Kate and a frustrated Yolanda staring after him as he made his way to the annex.

With Marc no longer beside her Kate moved around the group and continued to mingle. Although the conversation flowed she missed his presence. These were his friends, his colleagues. And it was brought home to her just how far apart she was on a social scale from these people. Here was high finance and wealth beyond her imagination, and although she wasn't intimidated by their affluence, she felt dwarfed by these mega-moguls and their wives.

About twenty minutes had passed before Marc's absence became noticeable. Several people asked Kate where her fiancé was, so she thought it best if she went in search of him. The Anistons were waiting to start the meal and Marc's absence was holding things up. Going over to Robyn, Kate explained that she was going to check on Marc to see what was delaying him, and that she wouldn't be long.

"I hadn't noticed that Marc's not back yet," Robyn said diplomatically.

"I expect you want to serve lunch," Kate said, glancing at her watch. "It's getting late, and Marc did said to start the meal when you're ready..."

"Oh, there's no rush," Robyn said. "Jeff can push up the start time of the meeting. A longer break might do everyone some good. And we can wait for the two of you to join us. I expect Marc's still changing."

"Then I think I'd better hurry him along, don't you?"

Leaving Robyn to look after her guests, Kate made her way through the garden toward the annex. When she reached the annex she opened the door and walked straight through to the bedroom where she expected to find Marc. And she did. He was coming out of the steamy en-suite bathroom. It was obvious he was fresh from a recent shower, and with his head bent he was hurriedly throwing on a clean shirt.

His shirt was open, exposing him to the waist, and his bronzed chest and rippling muscles were shown off to perfection. He looked strong and sexy, like a dark panther.

Marc concentrated on fastening the shirt's buttons, then glanced up and immediately took in the scene that was staged before him.

Yolanda was lying beneath the sheets and was obviously naked, while Kate was leaning against the doorframe seeking support. Transfixed and shaking from shock, a tight crushing pain caught at Kate's heart.

The sight of Yolanda stretched out on the bed, the very same bed she'd shared with Marc, brought memories flooding back of that morning. Was it only this morning she'd been in that very same position? Had she not lain in the same bed, naked and ready for him?

Feeling betrayed, a tidal wave of emotion rushed over Kate. She was wounded, devastated beyond belief, and when Marc looked at her she knew he saw the hurt and pain in her eyes.

"It's not what it seems," Marc said quickly, trying to rationalize the situation.

"It's exactly what it seems," she told him, and gradually she felt the shock dissolving as the rage began to build deep inside.

She was coming back to life and her heart was resuming its beat. Once more blood began to surge through her veins, and her feet were firmly on the ground. Reality was returning, and she was seeing Marc for what he was.

"I always suspected you used women for sex, and you've proved me right," she said coldly, with an aching anguish in her voice. "What am I to you, Marc? Was I just a bed partner you needed for the weekend? An easy lay? Someone to share the night with?"

"Kate..." He paused and took a deep breath before continuing. "Look, I'm not used to explaining my actions. I'm not answerable to you or to anyone. But I promise you…it wasn't like that."

"I thought we had something special," Kate said, remembering their hot, passionate night together.

"Of course we've got something special. You are special," he persisted, giving Kate a glimmer of hope.

Then from the bed came the sound of taunting laughter. Throwing back her head, Yolanda released a mocking gurgle of mirth as she lay listening to the conversation between Marc and Kate.

"Kate, my dear..." Yolanda said spitefully. "Marc says the same thing to all of us. Once he's taken what he wants, we all become *special* to him."

Yolanda was destroying Kate's last chance of happiness. The knife was turning and doubt was stabbing at Kate's wounded heart.

Kate knew Marc was barely controlling his temper. He walked over to the bed, where, towering above Yolanda, he spat out a stream of vicious, harsh, angry words.

But for Kate his protests had come too late. Her heart was heavy and she was sadly disillusioned. She knew she had to leave…and she had to leave now. While his back was turned, she turned and walked away.

Hurrying through the lounge, Kate spotted her packed suitcases and handbag in a corner near the sofa where she'd left them earlier that morning. She and Marc were supposed to be returning to Paris that night and her things had been left ready for collection. But right now she didn't have the time or the strength to carry the suitcases to the main house. Instead, as she rushed from the annex she took only her handbag containing her passport with her.

If she was to make a speedy exit, the suitcases containing all the new clothes Marc had given her would have to be left behind. And she didn't care. She wanted nothing of his. She wanted no reminders of Marc and their weekend together.

Kate knew she had to find a way to leave the Anistons' home before Marc could stop her. She couldn't stay a moment longer, because it would be torture to watch Yolanda dig her claws into Marc and take possession.

Kate couldn't—and wouldn't—sit on the sidelines observing, watching as the two played out their torrid affair. Cade might be able to tolerate seeing them together, but she couldn't. The weekend was over. It had finished early, and with her eyes full of tears Kate nearly collided with Robyn as she ran into the house.

Seeing the tears, Robyn hastily pulled Kate into one of the side rooms, away from prying eyes and onlookers.

"What is it? What's happened?" Robyn asked, her voice full of concern.

"I'm sorry, Robyn. I can't stay. I have to leave."

"What's wrong? Has something happened at home?"

Kate took some deep, calming breaths as she searched in her bag for a tissue to wipe away her tears. "No. I'll be fine, but I have to leave now before Marc finds me."

"Where is he? Shall I fetch him?"

"No...please don't. He's still at the annex with...with Yolanda."

"Yolanda?" Robyn asked suspiciously.

Then the expression on Robyn's face changed, and Kate knew there was no need for her to say any more—Robyn had put two and two together.

"Kate, it's not what it seems...it can't be. Marc once told me he never has and he never would touch Yolanda with a barge pole. And I know he wouldn't."

"But he has. I saw them together," Kate said, choking back tears.

Gulping deep breaths of air, she quickly took control of her emotions. She had to be strong. She wouldn't crumble. She wouldn't let Marc and Yolanda get the better of her.

"You're wrong. You must be. Marc would never betray Cade. And he would never betray you. I know he wouldn't," Robyn insisted.

"Me?"

"Yes, you. I've known Marc for years and until now I've never known him to be in a serious relationship. The two of you are engaged. He would never betray that trust."

"But he has. And he's betrayed his friendship with Cade. Marc's with Yolanda now. She's lying naked in the same bed Marc and I shared." Kate was visibly shaking.

"There has to be a reason why she was there," Robyn persisted. "Stay and talk to Marc...please."

"I can't."

"But you have to stay. You're supposed to be joining the company this afternoon. You're supposed to be signing the Castell-Aniston contract."

"That's another thing I can't do. Don't you see it would be impossible? I simply can't go into business with Marc and Jeff. Now that I've seen Marc with Yolanda I couldn't see him every day knowing he was with her...sleeping with her...making love with her. I couldn't."

Finding Marc and Yolanda together in such a way, it became clear to her that she could no longer join Marc and Jeff in their business venture. The situation would be unbearable. It would be too awkward.

She needed total independence from Marc Castell and his company, and she wanted no ties and no emotional involvement with him...ever again. It wasn't until that moment Kate realized how possessively jealous she could be. It would be excruciating to watch Yolanda or any other woman reveling in their relationship with Marc. No, she couldn't join Castell and Aniston. It would be too much of a torture.

"Would you offer Jeff my apologies? Say goodbye for me and explain as much as you can about..."

"Don't worry about Jeff. I can manage him. It's Marc I'm worried about."

Kate shrugged her shoulders, unconcerned. "That's one person no one need ever worry about. Marc will always land on his feet," Kate said bitingly. She was holding back her bitter rage with difficulty.

"But he's still a man—" Robyn persisted, defending Marc in his absence.

"I don't care about Marc, and I don't care what he does. He's made his bed and he can lie in it...with or without Yolanda." There was a vengeful hostility in Kate's voice that had never been there before.

"You're wrong. He cares about *you*. I'm sure he does. I've seen the way he looks at you."

Kate didn't want to hear anything more about Marc, and Robyn's protests were to no avail, they were falling on deaf ears.

"Robyn, do you think you could call me a cab? Please. I need to get to the airport, and if I'm to catch a flight before Marc finds me, I have to leave now."

"What shall I tell him?"

"Nothing. There's no need to tell him anything." Then thinking about it, Kate said, "If you must tell him something, say I had to return to England...and that I'm going to Daniel. That ought to get the message across that I never want to see him again."

"Daniel?" asked Robyn curiously.

"Marc will understand." And on those words the subject of Marc was closed.

Realizing Kate was determined to leave, Robyn said, "I'll go find Jeff's secretary and get him to make arrangements for your journey. You'll need the limousine, and we'll see to it that you get put on the first available flight back to England."

"Thanks, Robyn."

Robyn left the room and when she returned, smiling, everything had been organized, and Kate knew she would soon be away from Marc and out of his reach.

"One of the perks of being in the travel business is that I get to tell our pilots and boarding crew what to do," Robyn said. "Your seat has been booked, and the flight will take you straight into Heathrow."

Kate gave Robyn a warm hug and a shaky kiss on the cheek. Not everyone would have been as kind or understanding as Robyn had been to a new friend. And Kate now considered Robyn to be a true friend. Robyn hadn't judged her for her action, nor criticized her. She had only tried to help as best she could.

"Thank you so much for everything," Kate said, expressing her gratitude. "I'm sorry to be leaving in such a way, but I feel I have to."

"This tiff with Marc will soon blow over. I know it will. We all go through these phases when we doubt one another's love. I really think you should stay. Running away isn't going to solve anything. Are you sure you can't stay?" Robyn asked.

"I'm sure."

Robyn tried one last time to persuade Kate not to climb into the waiting limo but to no avail. Kate needed space and time alone.

"We'll have to stay in touch, Kate."

"Of course...I promise." And then Kate was whisked off to the airport before Marc had a chance to stop her.

* * * *

Once back in England Kate decided she needed to get out of London for a couple of weeks. She had to go someplace where she would feel safe. Somewhere away from Marc, and somewhere where she would be out of reach of his powerful influence.

She submerged herself in her work. Any contract that came in involving work outside London she personally took on, leaving her capable staff to deal with the catering contracts in the city. Kate didn't want to risk running into Marc.

Since leaving France she'd received several calls from him on her cellphone, none of which she answered, and then one day there was silence. The silence only proved she'd been right all along. Marc didn't care. In her mind he'd given up too easily. Apart from the intense physical connection they'd shared she'd hoped they'd made an emotional connection. But how wrong could she have been?

Eventually she came to the conclusion that they'd had no meaningful joining of their minds or their bodies and that Marc, after using her, had simply discarded her and moved on.

The thought that she'd given herself to him and that he'd taken her, and made love to her for his own pleasure was torture. She believed that in true playboy style he'd exploited her innocent passion only to reject her and replace her with another woman.

Just thinking about him sent a sharp, agonizing pain clenching at her heart. There was a sense of hunger whenever she recalled the long, passionate night they had shared, and if she'd been deceived and hurt, she knew she had no one but herself to blame.

It took a while but eventually Kate began picking up the pieces of her shattered existence, and step by step she started living again. She knew she would survive. She had to.

CHAPTER TEN

After sealing the catering deal between Castell Hotels and Aniston Travel, Marc left Cannes as soon as he could and returned to England. Reaching London, he'd been unable to find Kate. Her trail had gone cold.

He'd tried her London address, and although Nikki had been there she'd refused to reveal Kate's whereabouts to him. The same thing happened when Marc went to McKenna Catering to make enquiries.

Patty had told him Kate was out of the city and was unavailable. Apparently strict instruction had been left that under no circumstances was she to be contacted, which meant both Nikki and Patty were keeping silent and were not divulging anything to anyone.

In other words, Kate was blocking Marc on all fronts, and it appeared she had more influence in getting what she wanted than the mega-tycoon with all his billions.

The only lifeline Marc had been thrown as far as Kate was concerned was from Robyn. The Anistons happened to be in London for the weekend. Jeff had come to the city on business, and Robyn was there for the shopping. Having arranged to meet for lunch, during the course of the meal Marc had swallowed his pride and asked Robyn for help.

Robyn, ever the romantic, was thrilled to be given the chance to try and get Marc and Kate back together again. Thinking of ways to reunite the two, she suggested perhaps there ought to be a party, and that Kate could handle the catering.

Marc was more than happy with the suggestion. He was also willing to lend his villa and his yacht, which was based in the South of France, to his friends for the occasion. In fact, he was prepared to do almost anything and go to any lengths if it brought Kate back into his life.

She was constantly in his thoughts. He wanted her. He was obsessed with her. He needed a cure for his craving, and he needed it fast.

Once Marc had given the go-ahead and said cost was no object, Robyn began planning the event; and when everything was more or less organized Kate was contacted.

* * * *

"Hi, Kate," Robyn said enthusiastically. "It's me, Robyn. I'm phoning because Jeff and I have an anniversary in about two weeks and we wondered if you could do an enormous favor and help us out."

"Great to hear from you, Robyn. What do you need help with?"

"Jeff and I would like to give a small party for about fifty of our closest friends," she explained. "We'd love it if you would cater the event. You would be much better at organizing the catering than I would. You'll know exactly what to do, and I'm sure I can trust you to make it a memorable occasion for us."

Kate didn't have the heart to refuse her friend...but she had to. She knew if she became involved with Robyn and Jeff and moved in their social circles it would be too risky. There was the likelihood that sometime, somehow, or somewhere, she'd run into Marc, and that was something she couldn't let happen. If she was to survive, she had to sever all contact with him and his world, and that included the Anistons.

The memory of what had happened in Cannes was too fresh. The wound was still open. And any reminder of Marc and the way he'd treated her still had the ability to hurt.

"Robyn, I'm honored you thought of me, truly I am, but I think you should find someone else to help with the party."

"Please, Kate. It would mean so much if you catered for us."

Kate was determined to refuse, but before she could voice her concerns Robyn explained the situation.

"We need you there, even if Marc can't be. It's such a shame he has to fly to Italy to finalize that deal. He said he'll be tied up the week of the party. Apparently, he's put the Italian meeting on hold once before, when he went to Paris. He had to recue someone's sister from a disastrous love affair or something along those lines. You know what Marc's like when a woman's involved, he never spills the beans, so I didn't get the full story. Anyway, it's a meeting he can't miss, not even for our anniversary. So he's not expected to be at the party. But you have to come, Kate. You must. We can't do it without you."

After a time Robyn's persuasive tactics began to wear Kate's resistance down, and having listened to Robyn's pleading for another ten minutes, and realizing Marc was going to be elsewhere, Kate eventually agreed to organize the party.

As soon as she said "yes" it seemed the world began revolving at twice its normal speed. Once again she was in the fast lane. She was in the world of the jet-set, the affluent, and the pleasure seekers of society...and it was invading her life for a second time.

Robyn promised someone would organize the journey for her, and said it would be an all flight trip. The island Kate was visiting was supposed to be vehicle free. Only shopkeepers and local residents were permitted transport. And within a week Kate found herself traveling to the South of France.

There had been a whirlwind plane flight across Europe followed by a short but intensive ride in a helicopter until Kate arrived safely and in style on the picturesque, idyllic Island of Hyères.

"We're here, *mademoiselle*," said the chopper pilot as they landed on a helipad near the harbor.

He switched off the motor and the blades of the chopper whirled to a stop. Without the sound of the engine there was a sudden deafening silence. Removing his headset, the pilot helped Kate unclip her safety belt. He told her to wait then went around the chopper to assist as she climbed out.

Kate was sticky from the heat, and as she carefully pulled her blouse away from the waistband of her skirt she was thankful for the cool breeze and fresh air blowing around her.

"I'll see your luggage gets to the villa, *mademoiselle*. I've been told you are to go to the harbor where there will be someone from the yacht to meet you."

"The yacht?"

"*Oui, mademoiselle*. I believe *Monsieur et Madame* Aniston have changed their plans. They are no longer staying in the villa. You are to go to the harbor and you will be taken to the yacht."

"And I don't suppose you know how I'm to get to the harbor?" she asked.

Flying in from the mainland Kate had seen *Îles d'Hyères* quite clearly as they approached. The clear blue waters and the white sandy beaches looked inviting, but from where she was standing she was unable to see which road she was to take in order to reach the harbor. The field in which the chopper had landed was hemmed in by shrubs and trees, and it was almost impossible for her to get her bearings.

"This way, *mademoiselle*. It's only a short distance. But if you like, I can go to the villa and see if I can borrow a car," the pilot offered.

"No thanks. There's no need," said Kate. "I'll be fine. Just point me in the right direction."

But instead of leaving her to make her own way to the harbor, the pilot escorted her along a dirt track and down an incline until they reached the quayside.

Gulls were screeching overhead, and the salty smell of the ocean filled her nostrils. When Robyn had warned her there were no vehicles on the island, except for local use, Kate hadn't realized exactly how empty of traffic the island would be. There was no real evidence of transport or proper roads, and for once she wished it was otherwise. Right now she could do with a lift. Even though it had only been a short stroll from the helipad to the waterfront, Kate could feel beads of perspiration trickling down her back from the slight exertion. She longed to get out of the clothes she was wearing and into a pair of shorts and t-shirt. It would be cooler, less formal, and she wouldn't look so out of place in these surroundings.

The harbor itself had a cluster of houses on the quayside, and as she looked around she thought the place seemed familiar. She couldn't quite put her finger on why that should be or what she recognized. It was just a vague feeling of having seen the place before.

When Kate was younger she'd traveled about France with her sister and parents, but she didn't think they had stayed on the *Îles d'Hyères* during those visits. Perhaps she'd seen this sleepy harbor in a holiday magazine, or someone might have shown her their holiday shots. She couldn't be sure, but it was certainly a picturesque scene before her and the place was indeed beautiful.

When the chopper had been flying overhead the pilot had used his radio to alert the crew of the yacht of their arrival, and as Kate and the pilot approached the quayside a motor launch was pulling in and tethering up alongside the harbor wall.

After Kate thanked the pilot, he handed her over to the yacht's crewman, and taking her seat on board the motor launch, she was soon speeding in the direction of a gigantic, luxury yacht anchored a short distance off shore. It was a striking vessel, and as they approached she could read the name plaque on the bow. The yacht was named *Chantal*.

Jeff and Robyn came onto the deck to welcome Kate on board. With no gangway for Kate to use, she gingerly climbed on board using a lowered boarding ladder, and upon reaching the immaculately varnished deck she was engulfed in a warm embrace from Robyn.

"I'm sorry for the change of plans," Robyn said. "We took the yacht out this morning and didn't make it back in time to catch the tide. The captain did warn us that if we wanted to dock quayside we'd have to return early, but I was so enjoying our trip that by the time Jeff insisted we turn about the tide had been and gone. It's entirely my fault. But let's hope the gangway is lowered when we have the party, otherwise we'll be in real trouble, won't we?"

"I hadn't realized you'd be having your party on board." Kate was surprised at this turn of events. She wasn't exactly sure what she'd expected when she'd agreed to cater for the Anistons, but a yacht hadn't been in the equation.

"Good to see you, Kate. You're looking fantastic as usual, but then you always do," Jeff said, diverting the conversation away from the subject of yachts.

"Thanks, Jeff. And it's lovely to see you too." Kate gave a wide smile as she planted an affectionate kiss on Jeff's cheek.

"Let's find somewhere with a bit of shade and have a drink, shall we? I expect you could do with something cool after that long journey," he said.

Kate was steered toward one of the seating areas on deck, and reclining back on a cushioned deck lounger, she had a great view of the harbor and the hills beyond.

"This really is a super vessel, but are you sure you want to have the party on board?"

"It's the ideal place to have a party, don't you think? Or do you think catering for fifty or so guests would be a problem? If so, we could always hold the party at the villa. Couldn't we, Jeff?"

"Sure," Jeff said, seemingly unconcerned about the party and its location.

"The yacht certainly has ample deck space, so it shouldn't be a problem," Kate said, thinking it would be easier to keep things as they were. "The pilot mentioned my luggage was to be taken to the villa, and I'm assuming that's where we're staying?"

"Uum...not quite. Jeff and I have decided that while we've got the yacht to ourselves we'll be sleeping on board," Robyn explained, and it was clear she was happy with this arrangement.

Jeff made a face that told Kate a different story.

"You know Robyn..." Jeff shrugged. "I have to do as I'm told."

Everyone knew Jeff wore the trousers in their relationship. But it was also known that Robyn didn't hesitate to use her special powers of persuasion when she wanted something from her husband.

"Darling, you wouldn't want to sleep at the villa alone, now would you? I'm sure you'd rather be with me. It will be so romantic sleeping on the water...won't it?" Robyn's seductive voice left no one in any doubt as to what she was jokingly referring to.

During the course of the morning Kate was shown around the yacht, and having inspected the various decks, she discovered the yacht was an exceptionally beautiful vessel. It was magnificent and looked large enough to entertain the expected VIP guests list and their security. There was plenty of room for socializing, both inside the vessel and outside on deck.

Knowing she was there to work, Kate also went below to check the galley kitchen and the yacht's kitchen crew. Everything was on hand that she could possibly need for the party, and it appeared this function was going to be easier to organize than she originally thought.

"There are at least six cabins that I know of," Robyn said, squeezing Kate's hand enthusiastically. "If someone wants to stay over, there's ample room to put them up. Marc's been such a darling allowing us to hold our party here. And then of course there's his villa which we can use. It's out of this world, but you obviously know that already. Being engaged to Marc you've undoubtedly been to the island many times."

"Marc?" Kate asked, and a terrifying feeling of dread surged from within. "You mean all this belongs to Marc?"

Kate knew Marc wasn't supposed to be at the party, but as soon as she realized the yacht on which the party was to be held belonged to him and that the villa where she was to stay was also his, a strong urge to run before things became too complicated overcame her.

If she'd known Marc was involved before she left London she would never have agreed to come to France. His involvement caused havoc and turmoil to the calmness and composure she'd found during the past couple of weeks while away from him. She thought the best solution for her would be to simply walk away from the situation now, before it was too late. And before she was hurt or emotionally wounded...again.

"Yes, everything here belongs to Marc. Didn't you know? I'm sorry, Kate. I thought you knew," Robyn said innocently.

"I didn't. I had no idea he had a place in the South of France. For some reason he's never brought me here."

Kate was being cautious. She wasn't sure how much Marc had revealed—or not revealed—about their fake engagement to the Anistons. Although she'd parted from Marc on bad terms, she didn't want to ruin his friendship with Jeff and Robyn by saying the wrong thing.

"Ohhh...so you've never seen his home?" Robyn asked.

"No...never."

"Well, if you look over there...that's the villa where you'll be staying. Isn't it beautiful?" Robyn was pointing toward the shore and there, nestled in the hillside above the tranquil blue water and a white sandy beach, was indeed a beautiful villa.

The villa was visually stunning, and Kate instantly recognized it as the villa pictured in the painting hung on the wall of Marc's penthouse apartment at the Castell Plaza Hotel. No wonder she thought she'd been there before. That was why the harbor seemed so familiar, and why she felt so *au fait* and in tune with her surroundings.

The villa was different in style from Castell House in Grosvenor Square. It didn't have the historic elegance of the Georgian building. Instead, it was a spectacular, modern building with a crisp, white exterior and clear-cut lines. Sparkling glass and gleaming chrome shone, dazzling the onlooker in the reflective sunlight. Elegant, stylish, and chic, it was magnificent...and out of this world.

Kate realized Marc was a man of many tastes. What she hadn't realized was exactly how diverse those tastes were. There was his Georgian classical home in England, his luxury penthouse suite in the heart of Paris, and now here in the South of France he had a modern, contemporary villa.

For the remainder of the evening as Kate sat with the Anistons on the polished deck of the yacht, plans were made for the party. And when the sun began to set and the air cooled, she was ferried back to the quayside and escorted the short distance to the villa.

Marc's housekeeper was there to welcome her, and after Kate had been shown the bedroom in which she would be sleeping, she was left to explore Marc's home at leisure.

Walking from room to room, she could feel his presence everywhere. He was there in everything she looked at. Seeing and touching his things reminded her of how different their lifestyles were, and suddenly all this display of luxury and wealth brought home exactly how dissimilar their worlds really were from one another.

Kate was thankful their relationship hadn't developed. If it had, she supposed there would always be boundaries between them. She'd never be able to cross the great divide and be part of his world. The social gap between them was too great.

As Kate thought of Marc, against her will her longing for Marc Castell, the self-centered, egotistical, yet utterly charming billion dollar mega-tycoon, grew stronger. She knew his faults, yet she still yearned for him. And even though she desired emotional revenge for the way he'd treated her, she discovered her physical craving for him was as strong as ever. After all these weeks she could still feel and taste the passion they shared. Her longing for him had never faded. In fact, her love had grown.

* * * *

Kate had a week to prepare for the party. There was plenty of time to buy supplies and find extra staff, but organizing the party wasn't her main concern.

One afternoon when Kate was relaxing with Robyn on one of the yacht's many sun decks, Robyn dropped a bombshell. She wanted to know what Kate would be wearing to the party.

Kate hadn't thought she'd be joining the actual party celebrations. She'd presumed she was in France solely in the capacity of caterer, so she hadn't brought anything with her that was suitable for such an occasion.

As a precaution she'd brought a couple of casual evening dresses with her from London, but they weren't designer, *haute couture* party gowns, and they certainly weren't suitable for the type of lavish party the Anistons were giving.

"I'd prefer to stay behind the scenes," Kate explained, resisting Robyn's invitation to be a guest. "It will be all hands on deck in the galley, and I won't have time to mingle."

She didn't want to overstep the social boundaries, and although the Anistons were treating her as a friend, they were also paying for her catering services. She was there to work.

"Nonsense, you're to be our guest," Robyn insisted firmly.

"It's not practical."

"It might not be practical, but Jeff and I want you at our party...as our friend. That's why we've asked you here. And as far as not having a dress, that's easily solved."

That afternoon, overriding all Kate's objections, Robyn commandeered Jeff's helicopter and the two women went on a shopping trip to a nearby city. The problem of what Kate was to wear was sorted, and with the shopping excursion completed they returned to the yacht loaded down with boxes and packages of elegant dresses and stylish shoes. Although the trip was a success, Kate's budget had been blown.

Looking at the heaped boxes piled on one of the loungers Robyn suggested that perhaps Kate should leave her new dress in one of the cabins below. That way on the night of the party, after preparing the food, Kate could shower and change on board, avoiding an unnecessary trip back to the villa. Thinking it a good idea, Kate followed Robyn below decks to see where she could store her things, but when they arrived at one of the cabins Kate suddenly took a turn for the worse. She became dizzy and unwell, and with her world spinning before her eyes Kate reached for a nearby bed and slumped thankfully down onto it.

"What's wrong? What is it?" Robyn asked as she propped a pillow behind Kate's back for support.

"I'm all right. It'll pass," Kate said, trying to reassure Robyn that everything was fine.

"You look dreadful. I'll ask Jeff to send for a doctor."

"No, don't...please. I'll be all right." And as Kate said those words she started retching and made a quick dash for the bathroom.

"What's brought this on?" Robyn asked as she followed Kate into the en-suite. "It can't be food poisoning. We both ate the same thing at lunch."

Then, seeing the look in Kate's eye, the penny dropped.

"You mean..." Robyn stared at Kate in wonder and amazement.

Kate nodded. "I think so," she confessed.

A couple of times Kate had felt nauseous when she'd been on board the yacht, but she'd thought it was motion sickness from the waves lapping against the hull. Now she suspected differently. Putting all the facts together—the time she'd made love in the shower with Marc without protection and how long it had been since her last menstrual cycle—she was coming to an obvious conclusion...she might be pregnant. She could think of no other reason why she was feeling this way, and the only logical thing for her to do would be to take a test and find out if she was carrying Marc's child.

"That's wonderful news, Kate," Robyn said enthusiastically. "Marc will be so thrilled."

A shiver of horror ran up and down Kate's spine at the thought of Marc finding out about the baby. "No, please...you can't tell him. You mustn't tell him. He's not to know."

"Why not? He'll be delighted."

Kate had no idea if Marc wanted children or not. She didn't think he did, but then again they hadn't been together long enough to talk about having a child. They'd only been together long enough to make one.

"We've never discussed having a family," Kate explained.

"But Marc loves children."

"I don't want him to know. It would complicate things," she said unwaveringly.

Kate was determined he wasn't to know about her condition. She couldn't excuse him for the way he'd rejected her on that fateful day in Cannes. Neither could she forget he'd gone straight from being with her into Yolanda's arms. No, it was too hard for her to show him mercy. He'd wounded her too deeply for forgiveness.

"I know without a doubt that once Marc finds out I'm pregnant he won't let me keep the baby. I'll have no say in the matter. One way or another he will find a way to take my child from me." And on those words Kate let out a deep, exhausted sigh.

"What do you mean he won't let you keep the baby?" Robyn asked, shocked and surprised.

"He's bound to think he can raise our child better than I can, and he'd be right. He has more to give. There's no way I can compete with what he has to offer a child. Marc's wealth, his position in life, his—"

"Stop," Robyn said sternly, gaining Kate's full attention. "I don't what to hear another word about Marc taking your child. Now you listen to me. You have a lot to offer your unborn baby. You have stability, devotion, and you can offer a mother's love, which Marc can't give. Don't for one minute doubt yourself, and don't you dare compare what Marc has to offer to what you have to give."

"Oh, Robyn...I love the way you believe in me."

"Of course I believe in you. Now believe in yourself."

"I will. I shall. But you have to promise me you won't tell Marc. Please, Robyn, promise you won't mention the baby."

"Are you sure you and Marc won't be getting back together?"

"I can't see it happening."

"What will you do when the baby's born?" Robyn asked.

"I'll manage," Kate said. "I have to."

And she knew she would. She was strong. She could survive. With or without Marc, she would make it.

Back on deck and with the sun about to set on the horizon, Kate thought it was time to return to the villa for the night. Seeing Robyn cuddling next to her husband as they sat entwined on a divan was too much for her. She felt alone and isolated, and she soon found an excuse to make a timely exit.

It was strange staying at the villa knowing she was sleeping under Marc's roof. The opulence of her surroundings was absolutely breath-taking. Never before had she had an opportunity to enjoy such luxury and in such a beautiful setting. It was like paradise. Her every wish was catered for even before she knew what she required. But something was missing and that something was a person...*Marc*.

* * * *

When the night of the party arrived it was all systems go, and Kate was in her element. She loved cooking and preparing buffets. She thrived on events like these, and it was an ideal showcase for her skills.

A ferry had been chartered to bring guests to and from the mainland, and gradually the select party of fifty guests were transferred from the ferry onto the yacht. Couples dressed in designer finery and gleaming with precious jewels were trickling on board. With mood lighting in place and unobtrusive music playing in the background the party was soon in full swing.

Everything was up and running smoothly, and Kate, happy with the way the catering personnel were responding to the needs of the guests, thought the time was right for her to join in with the celebrations. Going below to change, she found not only her evening gown in the spare cabin, but her luggage had also been brought over from the villa.

Kate had decided to spend the night on board and supervise the clean-up operation in the morning. She could then say goodbye to the Anistons, and it would be a simple matter to hitch a fifteen-minute ride on the ferry to the mainland before heading for the airport in time to catch the next available flight to England. Making her escape sooner rather than later would also mean she'd avoid the possibility of running into Marc should he happen to make an unexpected appearance.

Taking a quick shower and applying her makeup, Kate was ready in next to no time. This evening she was wearing her hair piled high on top of her head. It was cooler, and it also showed off her off-the-shoulder dress to its best advantage. As she moved around the cabin, the dark blue taffeta gown with its wide skirt and silken folds swished and rustled sensually against her legs, making her feel like a truly desirable woman.

Having put the finishing touches on her makeup Kate went back on deck, greeted by the sound of clinking glasses and shouts of laughter as the guests offered a toast to Robyn and Jeff. It was a moment of celebration, and after the cheering and clapping had finished, couples followed Jeff and Robyn's lead and took to the dance floor. There was no doubt the party was going to be a success, and it had only just begun.

Kate hadn't realized the captain was going to take the yacht out to sea, but when the engines started and they were sailing along the coast of the glistening French Riviera she knew it was the right place to be.

Couples were swaying to the music, and romance was in the air. Night was falling, and as the sparkling lights of coastal villages shined toward them Kate thought she could almost hear friendly shouts of "*hello*" from the shoreline as they went sailing past.

It was a fairy-tale dream.

Feeling suddenly lonely and slightly out of place, Kate moved toward the stern of the yacht. Finding a secluded spot away from the partying crowd, she sat down on a cushioned bench that was sheltered from the cool of the evening breeze, and then she saw him.

In the shadows, leaning casually against the ship's rails was a familiar figure. *Marc* was there...on board.

How long he'd been standing there she didn't know. He slowly straightened and began coming toward her. Once he was standing directly in front of her, their gazes locked, and she felt a rush of familiar longing.

Dressed in a black tuxedo, Marc looked devastatingly handsome. Her heart flipped and her pulse rate soared at the sight of him.

"May I?" he asked.

Without waiting for an answer, he sat down, placing an arm along the backrest of the seat. Marc moved carefully, as if he were afraid he might scare her. The intimate contact of his arm as his sleeve brushed against her skin sent ripples of forbidden excitement racing through her.

Marc wasn't supposed to be in France. He was supposed to be in Italy. If she'd known he was on board the yacht before they set sail, she would have run and kept on running as far away from him as possible.

* * * *

The look in Kate's eyes made it clear to Marc that she wanted to run away, and keep running. But it wouldn't have made any difference if she had, because Marc was determined to pursue her relentlessly until he got what he wanted. He was hungry for the taste and feel of her body, and he wanted once again the passion they had shared.

Marc Castell, the man who was a "love them and leave them" type of guy, wanted a relationship.

"What do you think of the party so far?" he asked nonchalantly. He was testing the waters and trying to ease the sizzling tension that was between them. "Are you having a good time?"

"Why are you here, Marc? You're supposed to be in Italy. If I had known you would be here, I never would have come to France."

"That was what I was afraid of. I knew if I'd asked you to be here you wouldn't have come. And I would still be scouring London trying to find you. I asked Robyn and Jeff not to tell you I'd be at their party tonight."

"But why?" she asked.

"Why what? Why am I here? Or why would I search London?"

"Both," she said.

"The answer is simple. It's because we have unfinished business. There are questions that need to be asked and answered."

"I don't need to ask you what you were doing with Yolanda. It was obvious. And even though you hurt me, you owe me no explanations."

"And you owe me no explanations concerning Daniel," he told her.

"Daniel?" She looked at him as if she had no idea who he was talking about.

"Yes, Daniel. Remember? Your boyfriend? The man you told Robyn you were leaving me for. You went back to England to be with him. Have you so many lovers you can't remember who you're with, or when?"

Marc didn't need to be told nothing had happened with Daniel. From the moment Robyn had given him Kate's private number he'd known how to find her. Using special contacts, he'd had her cellphone traced, and he'd known exactly where she was every minute of the day, twenty-four-seven. And private investigation showed there were no significant *others* in her life. Marc also discovered that until he stepped in and swept her off to Cannes for the weekend Kate had shown not the slightest interest in being with another man. According to the detective, Kate simply didn't have a past as far as men were concerned.

A blush stained Kate's cheeks, and Marc suspected it was due to embarrassment over the deception she'd played on him.

"I don't need to know about you and Daniel," he repeated. "It's not important. But I'd like to explain about what happened when you walked in on me and Yolanda."

Kate placed her fingers against his lips, stopping his words. "It's none of my business, Marc. I'm not your keeper. We're both free agents."

"But I'd like to tell you," he persisted.

Carefully, he pulled her against his side, and when she didn't resist he took a chance and started to explain.

* * * *

Even though the time wasn't right for explanations and Kate's emotions were still raw and she still hurt, she listened. And she believed him. When he told her it was as much of a surprise to him as it was to her to see Yolanda in the same bed they'd shared the night before, there was no doubt in Kate's mind he was telling the truth.

She listened until there was no more to tell and the memories of Yolanda and her deceitfulness were laid to rest. Yolanda could no longer come between them.

As the evening progressed Marc and Kate sat talking about things in general, and in due course Marc came around to the subject of the Castell-Aniston deal and how things were moving forward. At one point he even tried persuading her to accept the catering contract he once offered her, but she was having none of it.

"It wouldn't work, Marc. It's a really good offer for someone like me, and I do appreciate it, but there are too many difficulties to overcome. I now realize I have to channel my energies into my own business in London."

Thankfully, Marc didn't persist. He merely nodded and steered the conversation toward other neutral subjects until she looked around and pointed out that something was missing.

"Where are your henchmen?" she asked, referring to his bodyguards. "You usually travel with at least a platoon of reinforcements."

"Usually I do, but not tonight. When I'm staying on the island there's generally no need for security."

"But some of Robyn and Jeff's guests insisted on bringing their own protection with them. We had to have a security check done on all the catering personnel and the yacht's crew. I know for a fact some people refused to come to the party if safety measures weren't in place. Surely that would apply to you too."

"If we were in Italy, I'd consider having someone with me, but not here in France."

"Yet several bodyguards came with us when we went to Cannes."

"That was different. Cannes was a high-profile event, and there were several business people present that I didn't know. The people here tonight are Jeff and Robyn's friends, and that's good enough for me. Now, let's talk about something other than my bodyguards."

And that was the answer that Kate had to be content with.

With the moon and stars high in the sky, the yacht, having toured a long stretch of coastline, eventually began journeying back into harbor.

Kate didn't offer any resistance when Marc pulled her from the cushioned bench they were sitting on.

"Let's go find Jeff and Robyn. It's time to say goodnight before we go back to the villa for a nightcap," he said, and with their hands entwined, they left the seclusion of the stern behind them and moved along the deck toward the noise of the party.

Kate realized what Marc was suggesting wasn't a simple nightcap. The meaning behind his words was obvious. She knew if she went to the villa with him their night together would end with her sleeping in his arms, and knowing this she was prepared to face the consequences of her actions...but not tonight.

Tonight they would make love and she would relish in the delights of his touch once more. She was determined it would be a night of such sensual passion that Marc would be unable to forget her. And come morning when she left him, she wanted Marc to experience the torture of longing for her caresses in the same way she remembered longing for his.

But tonight was different. Tonight she was living only for the moment.

CHAPTER ELEVEN

Kate knew that all evening Marc had wanted her to himself. He'd been waiting patiently for this moment and finally, at last, they were alone with only the silence of the villa around them. Pulling aside the fine lace curtains which were covering the open French doors, Marc drew her outside into the darkness of the terrace, which was lit only by the moon.

In the distance the yacht's twinkling party lights could be seen dancing on the water, and the faint sound of music drifted toward them from the harbor. The only movement to catch the eye was the sway of the curtains as they caught in the breeze blowing in from the sea.

Along with a sweet-smelling fragrance of fresh blossoms from shrubs and perennials about them there was also the heady perfume of the wisteria that was growing against the lattice work on the terrace wall. Its fragrance dominated the night air, but it was a light, delicate, pleasing scent and it was stirring the senses.

"Hello, Miss McKenna. Welcome to my home," Marc whispered.

He was standing behind Kate. His breath was fanning her neck, and as he spoke Kate could sense his tension and feel his excitement. He was like a coiled spring waiting to be released, and although she wanted to prolong this moment she knew it would be impossible; he was too impatient.

Marc turned her to face him, cupped her face tenderly between his hands, and looked deeply into her eyes. It was *that look* that was Kate's undoing.

Briefly, she wondered if she ought to have stayed on board the yacht, but she knew deep in her heart she'd made the right decision to come here with Marc. Tonight there was no turning back. She'd come too far.

She was weakening and giving into him without a fight, and she knew why. Even though she had wanted revenge and retribution for the way he'd treated her, she discovered she still needed his touch as much as he needed hers. When Marc placed a long, lingering kiss on her lips, it was then that she found herself surrendering whole-heartedly, without reservation...because she had to.

"I've missed you," he said, and the loving smile he gave her was overwhelming.

"And I you," she confessed.

From the corner of her eye Kate saw the infinity pool. It was enticing her, and without any hesitation she pulled away from Marc. Unfastening the zipper on her taffeta gown, she allowed it to fall carelessly to the ground, and wearing only her silk panties, she walked toward the pool's edge.

At the shallow end there was a series of steps, and stepping into the pool, Kate gradually entered, walking into the enveloping water, and allowing it to cover her.

The water was refreshingly cool on her skin. Floating on her back, she looked up at Marc as he stood watching her. Opening her arms, she silently invited him to join her. He needed no second bidding. Stripping, he tossed his clothes on a nearby lounger and entered the pool, swimming slowly toward her.

"You're wearing too much," he said as he reached her.

His fingers were playing on her skin, tracing the outline of her scanty, silk panties. A smile reached her lips.

"Then take them off," she suggested daringly as she kept herself afloat.

Marc didn't need to be told twice. Hooking a finger beneath the thin thread of material, he yanked, pulling hard, and the delicate fabric fell away, leaving Kate totally naked and exposed.

Seizing her chance to elude him, she swam away until she reached the deep end of the pool. Unable to touch the bottom with her feet, Kate held onto a hand rail for support and then waited with impatience for Marc to join her. She didn't have long to wait. He came to her, and as he reached her, he clutched the rail behind her head and placed an arm firmly around her waist.

Roughly, he pulled her up against his side, and there was a raw hunger burning in his eyes. Every hard, muscular inch of him was pressed along the length of her body. Jammed against each other, fused as one, nothing was separating them.

Kate could hold back no longer, and a sound of longing escaped her throat. She was almost at the point of coming, but she had to wait and take it slow. Marc wasn't ready for her…not yet.

She knew he was aroused because his manhood was hard and stiff, and although his body was ready to take her, she wanted to make him yearn for her so much that it hurt to the core of his being...just as it had hurt her when they'd been together making love in Cannes.

As Kate ran her finger through his damp hair their gazes locked and she could see his urgent need in his eyes. He was ready to plunge deep into her, fill her, and explode inside her. She knew he wanted to stretch her and make her his, but tonight she was the one who was setting the pace, and it was a pace that was too slow for Marc's liking. The persistent throb of his shaft told her he was ready, but she continued playing with him, teasing him, and to a certain extent...resisting him.

Unable to wait any longer, Marc's fingers began probing, seeking the soft divide between her legs, and when she shifted position it was Marc's turn to hold onto the rail and keep them above water. She was now in control and he was going to be a slave to her wishes.

As he supported them both in the water, her hands slid around his back, and clinging to him, she began grinding her body against his. Locking her legs around his waist, she clamped down tightly, wanting to get closer, longing to be filled by his hard rod. With the erotic feel of the water splashing against her skin and Marc's gentle caresses as he stroked between her legs, it was difficult for her to concentrate.

"I need to feel and see you," he whispered.

His voice was low and his French accent was heavily pronounced, but the urgency in his words left her with no doubt that she was affecting him. Deciding it was time to launch her attack, and feeling daringly provocative, Kate took the lead in their lovemaking. She captured his mouth with hers. Parting his lips with her tongue, she explored, deepening their kiss until he let out a moan of sexual hunger.

Breathless with anticipation, she clasped her arms around his neck for support. Then lowering herself slowly downward until she was hovering above his thick rod, she delayed the final moment of penetration. She was tempting him, and although she was rubbing his stiff, eager manhood between her legs she wasn't allowing him to enter...not yet. She was holding back, making him wait.

She nipped his earlobe gently with her teeth, and she felt him shudder. Never the aggressor or instigator in a relationship, Kate was relishing her newfound role. Then, breaking away, she swam to the shallow end of the pool and climbed out. She was expecting Marc to follow, and he did.

Marc was impatient, and when he lifted her up into his strong arms, she wound hers around his neck and pressed her breasts firmly against his hard chest. He felt so good...so solid...so sexy.

Dripping water from their dip in the pool, he carried her to one of the poolside divans and laid her down before joining her amid a pile of soft, quilted cushions. The divan was large enough to easily accommodate two people.

At the foot of the divan there was a cotton throw, and pulling the throw up around them, he wrapped her lovingly in its folds, shielding her and protecting her from the cool night air blowing in from the sea.

Both Marc and Kate were oblivious to everything around them...except each other. Naked in one another's arms, they were in the open beneath the night sky with only the glowing light of the moon shining down on them.

Kate couldn't help herself, and slowly, she began returning his passionate kisses. But when his embrace became urgent, his need to touch her more intense, she wanted all he was willing to give. She wasn't holding back, and at that moment she knew she was in danger of losing control.

As their sexual tension snowballed she couldn't wait any longer. She was never more thankful than when Marc pushed the throw that was covering them down to her waist and started caressing her breasts. Her breasts fitted perfectly in his strong, masculine hands, and when his thumb and fingers began playing with her nipples they instantly hardened into firm, erect peaks at his touch. Marc nipped and teased gently at her nipples with his teeth, and she trembled with aching delight while crying out his name.

"Please, Marc," she whimpered in delirious agony.

"Please what?" he asked while continuing to explore her body with his tongue.

Kate's urgent groans of desire were increasing. When she ran her fingers through his thick, damp hair and across the rippling muscles of his back, she wanted nothing more than for Marc to enter her, take her, and make her his.

"Do I kiss you better than Daniel does?" he asked tantalizingly.

"Please, Marc. Let's leave Daniel out of this."

Her mind was on other things—things like how Marc was making her feel and what he was going to do to her. And right now she couldn't think straight.

She knew that at some point she would have to confess the truth to Marc about Daniel, but now wasn't the right time. Kate needed to hold onto the illusion of Daniel being her boyfriend a little longer. Daniel was her protective shield against Marc's seductive onslaught. She would be safe from any emotional hurt Marc could inflict if she let him believe there was another man in her life. But she couldn't think about the problem of Daniel, or for that matter Yolanda, right now. All she could think about was Marc and what he was doing to her body.

With his fingers rubbing the hard buds of her nipples, the peaks were aching with longing. Every cell in her body was alive with desire, and she couldn't help but quiver in anticipation of what was to come. She needed him desperately. She was hot and aching for him, and she wanted him deep inside of her, filling her, stretching her, but most of all she wanted Marc to make love to her like there was no tomorrow.

"You taste so good. So very good," he whispered in his low voice as his lips returned once more to the tips of her aching breasts.

Her body jerked in delicious, erotic spasms. With the briefest of caresses he had her crying out in agonizing pleasure. She was his to command.

It shouldn't be like this, she thought as she felt her pulse quicken and her heart race. Her plan was to make Marc want her. She should be the one making love to him. It should be her seducing and enticing him into the realms of sensual delights, not the other way around.

If she was going to tempt him, make him want her as she had wanted him, then she was going to have to pull out all the stops, and it was going to take a lot of determination and willpower on her part to act the seductress and seduce.

This was so out of character for her that she hardly recognized her true self. Never before had she made the first move when it came to making love to a man, yet tonight it was her turn to be the *femme fatale*. Kate wanted to show Marc what he'd missed all these weeks, and she wanted to give him something to remember when she left him tomorrow.

Running her hands up and down his back, she pulled him close against her body, and with her head thrown back and her neck invitingly arched, she was intent on bewitching him. As Marc kissed his way from her lips down the length of her body to her hips, his gentle, seeking kisses were her undoing. She was losing control, and gradually he began to take over.

Tossing the light cotton throw carelessly aside, Marc spread her legs wide, leaving her exposed and ready for his touch. The cool night air hit her burning skin, and then his hot breath and his wet tongue began working their magic. Kate was compliant as Marc took over, and willingly, she obeyed, yielding to his every demand.

His fingers were touching the tender flesh of her inner thighs, working toward the apex between her legs, and he was getting nearer and drawing closer to the core of her being. He was reaching for the spot between the sensitive folds of her womanhood, and with forceful, demanding fingers he searched for her clitoris. When Marc found the nub of hard tissue he pressed firmly, rubbing it with such vigor and intensity that she felt the burning heat deep within spread throughout her body.

Kate lifted her hips, giving him full access. On the verge of climaxing, she gasped, screaming his name as the muscles of her inner thighs tensed and quivered. No one had ever touched or excited her the way Marc did.

Spreading her legs wider still, he was exposing her, leaving everything open for his searching fingers to devour. His caresses sent electrifying shocks to her inner core, and she was on the point of spilling her juices, allowing them to flow.

The sharp, sweet pain as Marc continued to stroke her was torture. With an orgasm building and unable to hold back, she eventually released her nectar as wave after wave of an all-consuming orgasm hit her.

Over and over, she peaked as his fingers searched and probed. She was breathless, exhausted, and gasping with pleasure, but giving her no time to recover, once again his fingers explored between her folds.

"Marc..." she panted, hot with desire.

"You're so wet," he whispered.

A long finger slipped deep inside, joined by a second one. He was stretching her, preparing her for his erect rod and what was to come. The heel of his palm pressed into the mound of her sex, and as the ball of his thumb ran over the tip of her clitoris she jerked, unable to control the spasms that shook her body.

"Take it slow, Kate. There's no rush. We have all night."

"Please, Marc...I want you now," she begged. She couldn't get enough of him.

"Not yet, my love," he said as he looked into her eyes. "I want to make sure you're satisfied first. I know that once I'm inside you there will be no turning back...I won't be able to stop."

His softly spoken words made her tingle.

Reaching for his scattered clothing, Marc found a condom and sheathed himself. Kate considered telling him there was no need for protection, that she might already be pregnant, and that she might be carrying his child...but she held back. Now was not the time to reveal all.

Secretly, she thought it best if Marc didn't know about the baby. Custody for their child was a battle she wasn't prepared to fight at the moment. She knew that if they went head-to-head in any battle, Marc would win. He had more power, more influence, and more ability when it came to getting his way than she did. So when she left in the morning she intended to sever all ties with him. She was going to leave him ignorant of the fact he could be a father.

But that was tomorrow. Tonight, at this moment, she couldn't think straight. Not with his hot kisses driving her wild and his hard rod positioned at her open entrance. His strength surrounded her.

Kate couldn't wait. She was lost in her need of him. She'd reached such a fever pitch of longing that she wanted him now and wasn't prepared to delay the moment any longer.

Taking command, she pushed Marc onto his back and climbed over him. Kneeling on the divan, she wedged Marc firmly between her legs. She reached down and took his large, stiff rod in her hand and positioned him at her entrance. His engorged shaft was pressing against her slippery sex, and when her fingers touched him his rod stretched, enlarging even further.

"Tell me what you want me to do," she said huskily. "Shall I be gentle with you, or would you like it rough and tough?"

She was out of her depth. She had no idea what she was offering, but she was prepared to be wild and lustful if sweaty, grinding sex was what pleased him.

Lying under the stars on a bed of cushions, Kate felt extremely sensual. She wanted nothing more than to make passionate love to him. She had to have him, and she had to have him now.

Unable to stop herself, she trembled helplessly as Marc's fingers touched her inner thighs, caressing them. His seductive fingers were working their magic on her, and she was desperate for release.

"Slowly," he told her. "Let's take it nice and slow."

And they did.

Tilting her pelvis and thrusting her hips forward, Kate pulled Marc into her.

A little whimpering sound of pleasure escaped her. Sinking down onto his shaft, she stretched herself, opening up inch by inch until he filled her completely. Encased around his thick, hard length, she looked into his eyes and saw the satisfaction she was giving him. For once she knew she had the power to affect him, and it was a heady sensation.

"Kate," he groaned. Gently, he pulled her head down to meet his. "You taste so sweet."

There was an undeniable chemistry between them, there always had been, and as the excitement of their lovemaking danced like fire in her blood, she knew he experienced it too.

Marc was holding her hips and thrusting up into her. Letting out gasps of delight while savoring every assault, she ground her hips down onto him. Kneeling over Marc, and taking him deeper and deeper into her, she knew that what she was doing was right. This couldn't be wrong. This was meant to be.

Wildly on a tidal wave of multiple orgasms, she was riding him and it was heaven. There was no stopping as wave after wave of heated bliss surged through her body. With her inner muscles clamped hard around him, she squeezed until once again she had him groaning with pleasure.

Driven, she pressed closer to his body. As close as she could. Her mouth touched against his burning skin, and as desire surged through her she knew Marc was also on the verge of coming. Then he turned the tables on her. Still joined as one, he switched places and soon he had her beneath him and she was surrendering to his demands.

He forced her legs wide apart with his knees, and with every thrust of his shaft he was sinking deeper and deeper into her until he reached the hilt and could go no further. They were fused together as one.

Kate bucked and reared. Lifting her hips, she wanted to tempt him and provoke him into continuing…and he did. Her body convulsed with every strong, forceful thrust of his hips, and with her knees lifted and her legs wrapped firmly behind his waist, she was letting go of her inhibitions. With Marc grinding and pounding against her clitoris she could bear it no longer, and unable to hold back, she let out a rippling cry of exquisite fulfillment.

"Look at me, Kate," he commanded. "I want to see your pleasure as you climax. I need to know I'm satisfying you as I slide in and out." He was thrusting deeper and deeper into her. "Do you like this…and this?" he asked. "Do you like what I'm doing to you, Kate?"

Her groans of satisfaction told him how much he was pleasing her.

The pace of their lovemaking increased, and as the pounding of his shaft between her hot, wet folds intensified, he came long and hard, spilling his seed into her. Together they were taken over the edge of release into a sensual cascade of sexual bliss.

Exhausted yet satisfied, in the aftermath of their lovemaking they clung together as one among the scattered cushions on the divan. Perspiring and damp, they exchanged tender kisses until Marc began to withdraw.

"Uhh...don't move," she whispered against his shoulder. She'd wanted him to remain inside her. She didn't want to let him go. But it was too late, he had already slipped out of her and was standing beside the divan.

Wrapping the light cotton throw awkwardly around them both and lifting Kate up into his arms, Marc carried her toward the villa in the direction of his bedroom. The bedroom was a safe place to be, and it was a place where they could make love undisturbed until the sun rose on the horizon.

Kate knew there was no going back. She would be there with Marc until morning. In a few hours' time, when dawn broke, she would have to leave. But tonight she would allow herself one brief, passionate encounter with Marc, and that encounter would have to last a lifetime.

* * * *

When Kate saw the morning light creeping through the curtains she knew it was time to move. She had to be gone before Marc stirred. Slipping carefully out of bed so as not to disturb him, she crossed the room on tiptoes and entered the en-suite. Searching for something to wear and spying a bathrobe hanging on a peg, she hurriedly put it on and tied the robe's belt firmly around her waist.

Although she felt awkward about wearing one of Marc robes she decided it was her only option. She couldn't walk through the villa naked. The clothes she'd worn yesterday evening were still lying somewhere outside near the pool where they'd been discarded in the heat of their lovemaking. The rest of her personal belongings and luggage were on board the yacht, packed and waiting for her to collect them before she left for England.

With nothing to wear Kate had no alternative but to go in search of her evening gown and retrieve it from the pool area.

Leaving the en-suite and making her way silently back across the bedroom toward the door she had to pass Marc. He was still sleeping. His arms were spread out and the sheet had slid down, showing most of his bronzed torso. He looked so peaceful. And as he lay dead to the world it was almost as if he didn't have a care or any worries to disturb him.

The responsibility of his global empire obviously didn't keep Marc awake at night. Whereas she'd found herself spending many a restless night wondering if her business would survive. Although her business was prospering, it had taken several years of hard, intense work to achieve the efficiently run catering firm she now owned. Even though she was a successful business woman, at times there were still moments when she felt a sense of insecurity concerning her success. She warned herself there was always competition out there, and if she didn't keep the pressure on to push and promote the business she was sure a competitor would soon collar the niche in the market she'd carved for herself.

No, she couldn't rest on her laurels. She had to drive her business forward, and to do that she really ought to return to London. She'd been away from the city far too long. She needed to get back into the thick of things. Be where the action was. And she needed to run her business without fear of running into Marc.

Last night, if nothing else, she had achieved at least one thing—she had put her dread of meeting him unexpectedly to rest. She felt that once again she could meet Marc on equal footing.

If she bumped into him in the city and he happened to have another woman on his arm...well, it would break her heart, but she would survive.

Before leaving the bedroom she checked to see if her robe was securely tied. Looking up, she saw Marc was beginning to stirring. Turning onto his side, he slowly opened his eyes. Lifting his head, he looked across the room at her. He'd seen her, and she couldn't hide the fact she was on the point of departure.

"Come here, woman," he said, his voice still drowsy from sleep. "I haven't finished with you yet." An unmistakable blaze of desire burned in his eyes.

"I have to get dressed," she protested, but already she could feel herself beginning to melt. She was succumbing to the warm heat that was awakening between her legs.

"I said come here."

And as if drawn to a flame Kate walked toward the bed where Marc lay waiting for her.

Reaching out, he tugged the sash on the robe, breaking the knot, and the robe fell open, revealing her body still glowing from their recent lovemaking. She was exposed and showing all to the searching eyes that were devouring her. She could see a burning hunger in his dark eyes, and it was a hunger that equaled her own.

Kate knew that if she was going to leave him, now was the time. She had to leave while he still craved and desired her, and she was determined to be strong.

"I have to go to the yacht," she told him. "I have to speak to Robyn about the party and see if everything on board is all right."

"I doubt the Anistons are awake yet. They're probably in bed making love...as we ought to be." Marc pulled Kate down toward him and placed a kiss on her lips.

"The Anistons have the luxury to do as they wish...I don't. I have to work, and I also have to see that everything from the party has been cleared. That's my job. That's why I'm here," she said, reminding him that the party was the reason she'd agreed to come to France in the first place.

Marc rolled onto his back. Frustration was etched across his brow. "You mean the Aniston's needs are more important to you than mine? You're saying I take second place?"

She knew he was teasing her, but she also knew there was an element of possessiveness in his words.

"I didn't say that...but yes!" And she gave a lopsided grin.

"Damn it, woman," he said, and then burst into laughter. "All right, you win. This morning I'll take you to the yacht and you can do whatever you have to do...on one condition."

"Marc, you're always throwing conditions and ultimatums at me." Kate smiled, then sighed, after which she threw him an exasperated glance. "All right. Tell me...and that condition is?"

"The condition is that you're mine for the rest of the day, and I can do whatever I want with you."

One stolen day with Marc wouldn't hurt...would it?

One day and then she could be gone. She would be out of his life...forever.

Surely there could be no harm in that. But she knew there would be.

Once Marc thought he had a hold on her and that she would do whatever he wanted, her life would never be hers again. She would be Marc's. She would be irrevocably tied to him until he released her, and that would be when he'd found someone new to amuse himself with.

Kate started to think fast, and a plan began forming in her mind.

All her luggage and personal belongings were still on board the yacht. If she did as Marc suggested and let him take her to the yacht, she could either send him back to the villa on some pretext, or if she managed to collect her luggage without him knowing, she could leave France and escape back to England.

Her journey home had already been organized for today, so in theory nothing could be easier. All she had to do was get to the yacht, collect her belongings, and then catch the ferry to the mainland without Marc realizing she'd gone.

No problem.

"Deal," she told him with false confidence. "But for now I have to shower and find something to wear."

She was burning her bridges and taking the plunge.

"You look good in my bathrobe, but if you want something to wear, feel free to raid my cupboards," he offered.

It was an invitation she couldn't refuse. Leaving Marc lying in bed, she went to take a quick shower and after the shower she entered his dressing room in search of something to wear. She soon found what she was looking for.

Taking one of his silk shirts that were hanging in the closet, she put it on and rolled up the sleeves. With a chunky leather belt as an accessory she'd soon created a stylish shirtdress. All she had to do was find her shoes and she would be ready to go.

Propped up on his elbows, Marc was watching her every move as she went about the room dressing, and when she was ready she made her way toward the door.

"I'll see you downstairs," she told him.

"Don't I get a good-morning kiss from you?"

He was crooking his finger in her direction and pointing to the bed. With a smile, Kate walked over and leaned in to kiss his hungry lips.

That was her mistake.

She was within range and Marc reached out to take hold. With his hand around her waist, he captured her in his strong, muscular arms and pulled her down onto the bed. She landed on top of him as he lay between the rumpled, silken sheets.

"You know it would be easier if you didn't work," he said while raining gentle kisses wherever he could on her face and neck.

"I have to work. I have to earn a living."

"Thinking about it...you don't have to. There's a solution. Why don't you come and live with me?" he asked, smiling cheekily. He looked like a naughty boy offering a sticky sweet or his favorite toy to someone he liked.

Kate stared at Marc in amazement. He couldn't be serious. He'd left her speechless. Was he really suggesting she move in and live with him? That would be impossible. She had her own life to consider.

Since she'd gotten to know Marc she'd discovered he spent most of his time in France, and she was based in London. All her friends lived in London. Her family was there. And she couldn't leave Nikki to fend for herself, not at the moment. Nikki was still too vulnerable.

Then there was her career to consider. She had a rewarding and challenging business in London. Her career was something she valued, and it was something she wasn't prepared to relinquish, not even for Marc.

"Be practical, Marc. I can't do that."

"I am being practical. I'm being extremely practical. It would save you having to work, and it would save me having to be without you in my bed when I need you."

In a flash Marc went from being the little boy into a ravenous lover. The ardent, hungry look Kate had grown to know had appeared on his face and she knew he was aroused.

He planted impassioned kisses on her open mouth, and groaning softly against her ear, he whispered, "I need you, Kate."

Kate was left in no doubt that he did. Lying next to his strong, firm body she could feel his hard desire as he pressed against her. But she ignored his physical needs. She had to. She had to keep her mind focused. She had to concentrate.

Marc's unexpected offer had thrown her off-balance. Yesterday she'd wanted to make him suffer. She'd wanted to make him yearn for her so much that he couldn't bear to be without her...but that was yesterday. Now it appeared she'd succeeded and achieved her goal, and she felt no sense of accomplishment. She knew she couldn't accept Marc's offer.

"I'm honored," she said cautiously. "That's two offers you've made today. The first one was the use of your closet, and now you're offering me bed and board."

"Not just bed and board, Kate...I'm offering you my heart."

Marc's no-commitment rule had been broken. He was prepared to go all the way, but his offer was backfiring. It was only making Kate more determined to leave that morning before things really got out of hand.

She didn't know how to react to his offer. Yesterday when she thought about getting revenge for the way he'd treated her in Cannes she'd imagined him on his knees, begging her to stay, and now that he was she knew she couldn't accept his offer.

She wanted more from their relationship. She didn't want a temporary arrangement with any man, but especially not with Marc.

Kate knew that if she committed herself to being with him she wouldn't be able to walk away unscathed. Her heart would break. And then there was the baby.

She didn't know how Marc would react once he found out about their unborn child, but she couldn't tell him. She couldn't take the risk. He would think she was using the baby to get to him.

Once before he'd accused her of using blackmail to get at the Castells and the Castell fortune, and Kate didn't want to be placed in the same position of having to defend herself against those charges *again*. If he were to point the finger and hurdle unfounded accusations in her direction, she knew it would destroy her.

"I like my work," she told him, and it was true. She loved her work. "I like the challenge it offers, and I don't think I could *not* work."

"That's fine. I'll let you do what we originally agreed upon. You can come and work for me at Castell-Aniston as our caterer. Or if you don't want to do that, you can continue with your own company...as long as it doesn't interfere with us being together, day and night."

I'll let you! Had he really said *I'll let you*? The horror of his words was ringing in her ears. Who did this arrogant, conceited man think he was?

And in that moment Kate's emotions went from caring about hurting his sensibilities to a total, reckless disregard for his feelings. How dare he suggest he would *allow* her to work? She was seeing red. She was furious. How could she accept such an offer from such an egotistical, narcissistic, dictatorial man?

"We would make a great couple," he told her, and Kate knew it was such a bold statement coming from him. "We're good together."

"In bed, yes, but that's not a relationship, Marc." Although her voice was cool, inside she was fuming. "And to be honest, I don't know if I could live with you."

Judging by the look on his face, her words shocked him, but only briefly. Marc had too much self-assurance for Kate to knock him off-balance for long, and using his infinite charm he tried to persuade her otherwise. While seducing her with his words, his fingers weren't idle; they were teasingly running up and down her bare arm, sending shivers along her spine.

A deep heat was spreading between her legs, but now was not the time to allow her sexual desires to get the better of her. She had to keep a cool head. She'd had a taste of Marc's lifestyle. It was fast-paced, jet-set living, and for pleasure seekers with nothing better to do than spend their money. Knowing she might be pregnant, she didn't want to cope with that sort of existence. Now she had other priorities, other concerns, another person to worry about—their unborn child.

"I'm not losing this battle, Kate. There's too much at risk. So if you're not interested in moving in with me, I'll just have to up the stakes and play my next card."

"All right then…what's your next card?"

As she lay beside him, he took her face between his hands and looked deep into her eyes.

"Kate, over the past few weeks I've had time to think long and hard about how things are between us, and although we've only known each other such a short time, I think it's been long enough for me to get to know you and make a decision. We're good together. We're made for one another. And so I'm not asking you *just* to live with me and be my woman…I think it's about time we took *our next step*."

Gone was the playful teasing of earlier, and in its place was now such an intense look of desperation that anyone looking at him would know he was about to take a leap of faith into the unknown.

"Will you marry me, Kate?" he said tenderly, and then he waited patiently for her answer.

CHAPTER TWELVE

Marc's proposal was met with silence, coupled with a look of utter surprise on Kate's face.

"I can't marry you," she finally murmured. "It wouldn't be right."

"Think about it," he said. He had heard her rejection, but he had also seen the slight hesitation in her eyes and hoped he could change her mind.

A keen businessman, Marc knew when to push a client and apply the pressure and when to retreat. But Kate wasn't a client, and offering someone his hand in marriage wasn't something he'd done before. In truth, Marc was out of his depth.

"You don't have to decide now," he said. "And if it's where we're going to live that's bothering you, don't worry. We don't have to live here on *Îles d'Hyères* or in my London apartment. We can always buy a new place together. In fact, we can go wherever you wish."

Marc didn't have to say that money was no object, or that Kate needn't be concerned about having to work. With his wealth he could buy anything...but there was one thing he couldn't buy, and that was Kate's love.

"I can't, Marc," she said, and tears welled in her eyes. "It's a really good offer, and I'm sure you'll make someone very happy, but I never entered into this relationship with the idea of it being anything other than a brief fling. When you took me to Cannes I knew what you were offering was temporary. That was all right. It was fine. We had a great time, but you moved on, and since then I've moved on too. This weekend...well, things just happened and..."

"This weekend we've shared something special," he said forcefully, trying to convince her she was making the wrong decision.

"Yes, we did," she agreed, and then she glanced away, refusing to meet his gaze.

"You won't stay with me, will you?" he asked, but he already knew the answer.

"I can't. I'm sorry...*no*," she said, her words sounding strangled. Kate kissed Marc long and hard on the lips before climbing off the bed and leaving the room.

She pulled the door closed behind her, and for the first time ever...tycoon, billionaire Marc Castell was battling with feelings of rejection. Kate McKenna had turned him down. She had done the unheard of; she had said "*no*."

* * * *

Kate left the villa, making her way down to the harbor. The smell of the ocean filled the air, and gulls screeched overhead as baskets of fresh fish from the morning's catch were unloaded from trawlers.

Although it was early in the day several villagers, and even some of the Aniston's straggling guests, still dressed in their evening wear, were milling about on the quayside.

As Kate stood there gazing out at the ocean, her thoughts went back to her conversation with Marc. He had surprised her with his proposal. She'd never expected to hear the word *marriage* on his lips. She thought it was something he would never offer a woman. An affair, yes; but marriage, no.

He'd said he needed her, but he hadn't said he loved her, and she wasn't prepared to settle for anything less. She had to know the person she was going to spend the rest of her life with loved her. She had to hear him say the words *I love you,* and they had to be sincere. Kate loved him completely, but she couldn't accept his proposal, not without his love.

When she'd left him at the villa her heart had been breaking into a million pieces, but she'd been brave. And she'd walked away knowing it would be the last time she would ever see him.

The screeching of gulls grew louder, pulling her from her thoughts. It was time to go. She needed to go back home to England and try to put the pieces of her broken heart back together.

The *Chantal* was birthed along the quayside, and Kate climbed on board the yacht, giving Jeff and Robyn a wave in greeting as she did so.

Robyn came rushing forward from where she'd been sitting at the stern of the yacht, and it was obvious she wanted to know how things had gone after Kate left the party with Marc last night.

"I'm not stopping," Kate said, trying to avoid the sensitive subject of Marc. "I'm here to collect my things, and if I make the ferry, I'll be able to catch a connecting flight to England that's departing from the mainland within the next hour."

"You're leaving us so soon?" Robyn seemed surprised.

"Yes, but before I can leave I have to change."

"What's happened?" Robyn asked. "Why have you decided to suddenly disappear? I thought yesterday evening everything was sorted and things were now fine between the two of you."

"They are, sort of, but I have to go home. It's for the best." Kate didn't want to explain what had happened. Her emotions were still too raw.

Leaving the Anistons on deck, Kate went below. Her travel bags were still on board. They were packed and waiting to be collected. After retrieving a pair of jeans and a blouse suitable to wear on the journey, she slipped out of the makeshift shirtdress and changed.

When she was ready she found a steward and asked him to take her belongings to one of the mainland ferries on the quayside and leave them near the landing stage.

With that done, the only thing left for her to do was to give the *Chantal* a quick check over to make sure everything from the party had been cleared and was in place…then leave.

Kate had hoped to make a speedy escape from the Aniston's, but ten minutes later, when she was saying goodbye and thanking the captain and his crew for their support, Jeff and Robyn found her and insisted they accompanied her the short distance to the ferry.

Reaching the harbor-side, they all turned in surprise as they heard shouts from the hilltop. Marc was fast approaching. It seemed he was eager to have one last word with Kate. He'd obviously dressed in a hurry, throwing on a pair of shorts and a t-shirt, and he could have easily been mistaken for a casual tourist.

"And where do you think you're going?" he asked when he reached her. He was facing her square on, standing with his hands firmly on his hips, blocking the way, and preventing her from boarding the waiting ferry. It seemed Marc was determined to hinder her exodus.

"I'm on my way to Hyères. I'm returning to England," she told him defiantly.

Frustration welled in her throat and tears stung her eyes, and as much as she tried to avoid his enraged, smoldering stare she was compelled to look at him. Kate thought she'd said her final goodbye to Marc in the bedroom, but apparently she was wrong. It seemed he had plans of his own.

Marc reached for her, grabbing her by the shoulders. Pulling her around, he forced her to face him, and she could see the burning rage in his eyes.

"Please, Marc. You're hurting me."

"You're mine, Kate. You'll always be mine, and I'm not letting you go."

She heard the desperation in his voice and knew he was prepared to fight for their love, even if she wasn't. Tears of hopelessness rolled down her cheeks. Brushing the tears away, she swallowed hard.

"I can't marry you, Marc," she told him once again. Why wouldn't he take no for an answer? The man was too determined and too persistent...but he wouldn't be Marc if he wasn't. Marc Castell never took no for an answer.

"Then if you won't marry me...be my woman," he said.

Kate shook her head. She knew she couldn't allow herself to remain with him. She couldn't allow herself to want him with every fiber of her being, because if she did, her life would never be the same.

Her freedom would be gone. Her identity would vanish, and she would be forever changed.

"You can't go. I won't let you," he told her. He pulled her to the side, out of earshot of the Anistons, who were watching them with amazed expressions on their faces.

"Hey...steady on, Marc," Jeff called out warningly.

"Stay out of this, Jeff. This is between Kate and me."

"Not if it involves you putting your hands on her, it isn't."

Marc seemed to suddenly realize he was being somewhat brutal, and he released her. His fingers had left a scorching imprint on Kate's bare arms, and it was as if she had indeed been branded with his touch.

Kate looked up and gently stroked Marc's cheek. "I have to leave. Don't you see?" she said calmly. "I can't stay with you just because we have good sex every time we land in bed together."

"It's not *just* good sex," he corrected her. "It's great sex."

"All right then...great sex," she conceded, and there was a wry twist to her lips as she jokingly admitted he was right. "But don't you see we can never have a proper relationship? Your world is nothing like mine. We move in different social circles."

Placing a finger against her lips, he stopped her from saying any more.

"That's where I disagree." Marc had a worried frown of concern between his brows. "You were perfectly fine with my friends in Cannes. You were accepted and mingled with the crowd. I don't see what your problem is."

"Cannes was different," she explained. "That was business."

In Cannes she had coped. She'd handled the social tensions and mixed with his colleagues, but yesterday evening had been different. Yesterday she'd felt distanced from everyone. Perhaps it was because she'd been there in a professional capacity, or possibly it was because those people were on the yacht to be with the Anistons, but either way, there had been a barrier, and it was a barrier she didn't think she could overcome.

The ferry sounded its horn, indicating it was about to depart, and suddenly there was no more time to talk...she had to go.

Taking one last look around, Kate was overcome by emotion and tears began to well in her eyes. There was the breath-taking beauty of her surroundings. The shops and the cafés of the charming French harbor, the deep blue waves of the sea breaking on the white sandy beach, and then there was Marc's villa, nestled high on the green, grassy hillside.

Marc walked Kate over to her holdall and reluctantly picked it up. Putting his arm around her shoulders, he took her to the boarding platform, and among the crowd of scurrying passengers shuffling to board the ferry, he gave her one last long, lingering kiss.

"This isn't goodbye, Kate," he said, whispering the words which only Kate could hear. "I'm not letting you go. Not now that I've found you. I'll come looking for you in London, and one way or another I'm going to convince you we're meant for each other."

* * * *

As Marc released Kate from his arms a commotion occurred on the quayside.

A motor launch jetting into the harbor at high speed was causing a disturbance, while at the same time from one of the nearby cafés, two armed men appeared and began thoughtlessly pushing their way through the crowd of people waiting to board the ferry. The men were making a beeline straight for Marc.

Marc immediately knew what was happening—it was a kidnapping. Word must have gotten out that he was on the island and that he was unprotected. The opportunists had obviously seized the moment and were about to strike, because it wasn't every day a multi-billionaire was left unguarded and in such a vulnerable position that he was open to attack.

During the commotion, at some point, a shot was fired. Several people in the crowd screamed, and Marc looked over at Kate to discover that she had taken a bullet. She staggered backward, and as she was falling, Marc managed to catch her just before she hit the ground. Kate lay unconscious in his arms, and as panic and pandemonium broke out around them all he could do was hold her close.

As the crowd parted, fleeing in terror, the kidnappers were revealed, and the look of shock and disbelief on the shooter's face was clear to see. He was still holding the discharged weapon, and it was obvious it hadn't been his intention to fire. Apparently, the weapons had been there as a precautionary measure in case Marc had put up a fight. But now things had changed.

The air was filling with distressed shouts from the quayside and there was also the sound of a boat's engine revving nearby. The kidnappers, looking at one another, then at Kate's unmoving body in Marc's arms, obviously decided that they had no other option but to run. Dashing across the quayside, the men jumped without caution onto the motor launch and sped off, leaving the harbor at full blast without consideration for any persons or vessels within their path.

All this time, Kate lay lifeless in Marc's arms. For a second Marc thought he'd lost the one person in the world who meant everything to him. He thought she was dead. And then her eyes opened and she called out his name. Relief filled him. She was alive.

* * * *

"I thought I'd lost you, Kate." Marc's worry was clear to see.

Kate groaned as she tried to lift her head, but she couldn't. Dizzy from the after effects of the shooting, her head was spinning as she clung helplessly to Marc for support.

"Stay where you are. Don't move," Marc said, and there was deep concern in his voice.

"Where are they? Where's the gunman? Are you all right?" Even though it was Kate who'd been shot, her concern was for Marc.

Looking around, she searched for the shooter. She wanted to know if there was still danger or a threat of another attack. She was frightened for Marc and believed he was in jeopardy, risking his own life by staying with her here, out in the open. She wanted to get him to safety.

"I'm fine, and the kidnappers have gone. Everyone's all right...apart from you. Look at all this blood."

Kate had been hit in the shoulder, and a dark red stain was showing on her blouse. Panic was in Marc's eyes as he glanced at the spreading pool of blood then back to her face. Robyn gave Marc the scarf she'd been wearing, and he pressed it against Kate's shoulder in an attempt to stop the flow of blood, but a steady stream continued to trickle down her arm.

"We have to get a doctor," he called with urgency to anyone who was listening.

"What do you want me to do, Marc?" Jeff asked.

Marc stood, then lifting Kate high into his strong, powerful arms, he began walking determinedly in the direction of his home.

"I'm taking Kate back to the villa," he called out. "Jeff, if you or Robyn could phone through to the mainland for a doctor, that would be great. And I think it best if you get someone to send the chopper on ahead to meet the medical team and bring them to the island as soon as possible. Oh, and contact the authorities and tell them about the shooting, would you? Someone is going to pay for what's happened here today."

There was no mistaking the anger in Marc's voice. It left no doubt that someone's head would be rolling.

"Marc, put me down please." Kate wriggled weakly in his arms as she tried to escape his firm hold. "I'm quite able to walk, and I'm sure it's only a graze."

"And I'm sure it's more than a graze. You only have to see how much blood you're losing to know that."

Kate looked down at her shoulder, and as she did a jarring pain shot through her body, and once again she fell into a dead faint and lost consciousness in Marc's arms.

* * * *

Opening her eyes, Kate realized she was back at the villa in Marc's room and in Marc's bed. A woman with a stethoscope was standing over her, feeling for a pulse. A nurse dressed in a white uniform was hovering in the background.

"Hi, I'm Sandi Piaget, a doctor from one of the hospitals in Hyères. Mr. Castell called the medics in to take a look at you. He said you've been in a bit of a war zone."

"I'm fine really," Kate insisted, still groggy from the after effect of the shooting. "I have no idea why I passed out. I don't usually faint at the sight of blood."

"Well, that's good to hear." The doctor smiled reassuringly at Kate and made a note of something on a chart. "Although you were bleeding profusely, the bullet didn't enter. It was a deep scratch. As long as the wound doesn't become infected it will heal quickly, and you can take the dressing off in a couple of days. But for now everything seems to be okay, and except for that scratch on your shoulder, nothing appears to be wrong. But more importantly...how are you feeling?"

Kate looked at her shoulder and saw her wound had been bandaged.

"If it's only a scratch and nothing's seriously wrong, I'm sure I'll be all right. You see, I have to catch the ferry and a connecting flight back to England. If I don't leave now—"

"I'm afraid you won't be going anywhere today. The shooting has been a bit of a shock to your system, so I think it would be best if you stayed in bed for the rest of the day. Perhaps tomorrow you can get out of bed."

"But I have to get to the mainland," Kate insisted. She was worried, and knew she had to get away from Marc as soon as possible.

The doctor looked across at the nurse. "I think we'll give Miss McKenna that sedative now, nurse." Then, looking back at Kate, she said, "It will calm you and help you relax. You'll probably feel dozy and need to sleep, and when you awake—"

Kate clutched desperately at the doctor's arm. "No...please," she whispered, hoping no one outside the room could overhear what she was about to reveal. "No drugs...there's the baby to think of."

"You're pregnant?" the doctor asked, surprised.

"I'm not sure...I think so," Kate confessed. "I haven't taken a test, but it's been several months since…"

"I see," the doctor said. "Well, this puts a different slant on matters, doesn't it? What would you like us to do now, Miss McKenna? I don't have a test kit with me, but we can take a blood sample and have a pregnancy test done at the hospital. I can phone and let you know the result when it comes through, but that doesn't alter the fact you'll have to remain on bed rest for at least a day or two. In light of what you've told me, now more than ever, it is imperative you stay in bed. It's a precautionary measure. We wouldn't want you to take a chance and lose the baby...now would we?"

Kate sighed, knowing she couldn't argue with that.

Eventually the doctor and nurse left the room. Kate, overcome with emotion and a sense of frustration, turned on her side and allowed the tears that had been so long in coming to trickle down her cheeks. They fell silently onto the pillow.

She didn't hear the bedroom door open or the sound of Marc's footfall as he crossed the room to the bed. It was only when she felt the weight of his body next to her did she turn toward him, revealing the distress she knew was written clearly on her face.

Without saying a word, he pulled Kate into his arms and allowed her to release the tension that had been building over several months.

"Everything's such a mess, Marc," she sobbed. "I don't know what to do."

"Hush," he said soothingly. "You're here, Kate, and there's nothing you need do. Stay and recuperate, and if you're in the same frame of mind at the end of the week, we'll sort something out. Relax and get better. That's all I'm asking of you."

And as Kate lay secure in the safety of his arms she fell into a deep, tranquil sleep with Marc at her side.

* * * *

Their days at the villa fell into a routine. Kate slept in Marc's room while he moved into one of the guest bedrooms. Kate protested, saying he should have his own bedroom back, but he insisted she stayed where she was, and she agreed. She was sleeping where Marc usually slept, on his pillow, and if that was the closest she could get to him without actually being with him, then she was happy with that.

Mornings they rose early and had breakfast together near the pool. After a short swim they usually strolled down to the harbor and boarded the *Chantal* to have lunch or dinner with the Anistons.

It was a life of leisure, and it was a lifestyle that Kate wasn't used to. One evening when they were all sitting on deck watching the sun set on the horizon Kate broached the subject of returning to England.

"But surely you don't have to go back quite so soon," protested Robyn. "Not after Marc got in contact with Patty and told her to carry on looking after your business while you're away. Surely you can manage to stay another week or two."

"It's not fair to expect Patty to cope alone for so long. I know she's capable of looking after things without me having to be there, but in the long term there are decisions only I can make. It wouldn't be right to expect her to continue without me there for support."

"Oh, I used to think like that when I was starting Aniston's Travel," said Jeff jovially. "I felt I had to do everything myself, but Robyn put me right. She asked, 'What's the point of having senior staff if you don't make use of them and allow them show their potential?' And she was quite right. Weren't you, dear?"

Robyn nodded.

"Very sound advice," Marc said.

And so it was that Kate decided to delay her return to England for another week and to stay in contact with Patty via the internet and emails.

The days on the *Îles d'Hyères* whizzed by in a hazy blur—whereas in contrast, the warm summer nights were excruciatingly long and lonely.

Sometimes, in the middle of the night, she heard the sound of a door opening, followed by a splash from the pool outside her window. She daren't go out onto the balcony to glance over the balustrade and watch Marc plowing through the water. Instead, she lay in bed imagining the hard muscles of his body rippling as he swam to one side of the pool before turning and dipping, and moving back and forth, over and over to release his pent-up energy.

Kate wondered why Marc stayed on the island. She knew that like her he had business obligations and responsibilities he couldn't avoid. As the company director he couldn't shirk his duties for too long. But it was as if he'd put his life on hold…for her.

One day the housekeeper had been given the morning off and Kate, thinking she'd surprise Marc with breakfast on the terrace, was in the kitchen preparing a meal. Looking through the patio window, she saw him sitting outside, reading some papers and working on his laptop.

Kate was about to crack a couple of eggs into a pan when her cellphone rang. It was Doctor Sandi Piaget confirming what Kate had suspected—she was pregnant. Now all Kate had to do was to break the news to Marc and face the consequences. This week, being with him and getting to know the true Marc, she had come to the conclusion that if she was indeed carrying his child he had a right to know. She couldn't withhold that sort of information from him.

Switching off the stove, Kate turned around and was about to go and join him on the terrace when she saw Marc standing in the doorway watching her. She knew he'd heard part of her conversation with the doctor, and there was no mistaking the look he was giving her. He was expecting her to tell him what they'd discussed.

"Marc..." she began, and licked her lips that had suddenly become dry. "I have to tell you something, and I'm not sure how you're going to take it. There's no easy way to say this." Kate took a deep, calming breath before saying the words. "Marc…I'm pregnant."

He walked over to her, put his hands gently around her waist, and pulled her toward him. "I know," he whispered. "I've known for about a week. When you were shot and lay unconscious we were all concerned about you. Circumstances were such that Robyn was forced to tell me what she knew. She said you thought you might be pregnant. Our concern was for you and the baby."

"But you never said anything."

"No, I didn't. I wanted *you* to tell me. I had to hear the news from you, and I had to let you make up your own mind to do so. Although I might want to, I can't force you to stay with me because of our child."

"I would never stay with you for any other reason than because I love you." Kate took his face tenderly between her hands and looked deep into his eyes. "Marc, if I didn't love you with all my heart, I wouldn't be here."

"I know that, and that's what gives me hope that someday soon you will marry me and be truly mine, forever. Kate, I love you. Always. You know I do. So what do I have to do to make you mine?"

"I am yours. I'll always be yours," she said, and pulling him toward the bedroom, she showed him her love.

CHAPTER EPILOGUE

The hands on the clock told Kate it was nearly eight. The distant sound of the morning traffic could be heard coming from Grosvenor Square. Lying in bed, she thought about how her life had changed in such a short space of time. A year had passed since she'd first met Marc, and she was amazed at her good fortune. Life had just fallen into place.

Any difficulties she thought she might possibly have were always swept away by Marc's skillful handling of the situation. He always made things right. With Marc nothing was impossible, and her time with him was filled with laughter and joy.

Workwise, Kate had taken a back seat, and Patty and Daniel were now more or less running McKenna Catering. If Kate happened to be away from London, Patty managed the kitchen and catering staff while Daniel coped with a team of workers delivering the finished goods to customers at their door.

Nowadays Kate was often away from the city. She would sometimes accompany Marc on his frequent business trips and she would often join him when he visited one of the various Castell Hotels that were dotted all around the world.

In those moments Patty acted as an excellent stand-in for Kate. She helped Daniel and the McKenna Catering team run the business smoothly, ensuring everything went without a hitch. At the beginning of the year McKenna Catering had taken on the Castell-Aniston contract, and things in that department were flourishing.

The new arrangement suited everyone. Aniston Travel was happy, and the Castell Hotel Group was more than pleased with the service McKenna Catering provided for their day-trip guests. Even Cade and Yolanda, who were now living in Italy handling the account Marc had been negotiating, were happy. Generally, things couldn't be better.

Nikki and Eduardo were also thriving. They were both still working for the hotel and saw one another on a regular basis. Although nothing serious had yet developed between the two young people, they were good friends, and it seemed Kate's original fears concerning Eduardo's dishonorable intentions had been groundless. He was a great guy and had, as far as she could tell, a genuine affection for her sister. Nikki was proving she'd grown up enough to be able to look after herself and had moved out of their home in Eltham and into a flat of her own in Knightsbridge.

The alarm went off and Kate knew she couldn't lie beneath the covers any longer. She had things to do. Climbing out of bed, she walked to the bathroom, and after taking a shower, she got dressed, preparing herself for the day ahead.

Her days were always busy. She hardly had a moment to herself, and from the time she woke in the mornings to the time she crawled exhausted into bed next to Marc, she was constantly on the go. But it was a life she thoroughly enjoyed.

With her hair still damp from the shower she walked into the lounge, expecting to find Marc working at his desk. Sometimes in the morning, before the staff opened up the main office downstairs, he'd sit at his desk in the lounge, checking his emails and answering the post.

Realizing he wasn't there, Kate went over to the staircase and down the steps into the kitchen. The smell of fresh coffee hit her nose. Marc always said he could never function without a fresh brew first thing in the morning, and he'd obviously come downstairs early to make himself a pot.

"So, you've finally decided to stir and come in search of me, have you?" Marc was sitting at the breakfast bar. He reached out, and taking hold of Kate around the waist, and pulling her against him, he planted a long, hard kiss on her lips.

"No, not you," she said, returning his kiss with equal force. "I've come in search of our son." And as if on cue, having heard his mother's voice, a tiny infant positioned in a bouncing rocker propped next to Marc's laptop on the kitchen breakfast counter, began to cry.

"And how's my hungry boy?" she asked, lifting the baby out of his rocker.

* * * *

Something about Kate touched Marc in ways he'd never experienced with another woman. As he stood looking at her, with their son in her arms, he was amazed she was his to have and to hold.

He remembered the battle he'd fought, and eventually won, when she agreed to wear his ring and become his wife. Kate had insisted their wedding be a quiet ceremony with only family and close friends in attendance, and in its simplicity it had been more meaningful than anything he could have organized. But what surprised him most was the way he felt when she proudly showed off the plain silver wedding band he had given her. It fitted her slender finger so beautifully, and the symbol of their love told the world that she was at last truly his.

Marc still couldn't believe he'd found a woman who wanted more from him than the things his money could buy. He'd discovered all she was would willingly share with him was their home, his life, and the love of their child. Never before had someone given him everything for nothing. And perhaps in time he could persuade Kate to share more...he had so much to give. He knew that throughout their lives Kate was going to challenge him every step of the way. But knowing her as he did, it was a challenge he was happy to endure...forever.

* * * *

Passing their son—Luc, over for Marc to hold, Kate said, "I think both my boys are hungry and in need of feeding." And she set about preparing their meals.

When breakfast was over and with Luc fed and changed, Kate returned the sleeping baby to his crib in the nursery. With the baby monitor switched on she went back downstairs to find Marc.

While she'd been busy Marc had gone back to working on his laptop and was now concentrating on some document that was open and displayed on the screen in front of him.

Her heart was hammering with excitement as she squeezed herself between him and the worktop.

"Now that both my boys have been fed and looked after," she said and shot him a seductive glance, "I think it's time for *my* breakfast...please."

Tenderly, she began tasting his lips and running her fingers through his hair. Marc got the message and pulled her onto his lap. Slowly, he began releasing the buttons on her blouse, then almost immediately he stopped.

"What about Luc?" he asked, concerned.

"What about him?"

Kate was puzzled. She hadn't heard Luc cry out, and as far as she knew he was still fast asleep in his crib.

"Nothing. It's just that I thought..."

"What's wrong?" she asked. She could see Marc was genuinely worried about something.

"Should we? I mean, should you? You know—it's only been a few weeks since you've given birth. Are you sure you're ready for this?"

Kate chuckled as she realized why Marc was hesitant.

"Marc, it's been more than a few weeks. Luc is nearly two months old. Parents don't stop having sex just because they've had a baby. And yes, I'm ready."

"But isn't it too soon after..."

"No, Marc. It isn't too soon." And getting off Marc's lap, Kate pulled him toward the stairs.

"Well, let me tell you, Mrs. Castell," he said light-heartedly. "I think it's too soon for you to be climbing these stairs. You should be resting...in bed."

Lifting her into his arms, he carried her up the stairs, through the lounge, and into their bedroom.

Placing Kate on the bed, Marc joined her and pulled her into his arms.

"Don't you think we ought to be working?" he asked. "There's a pile of work waiting to be looked at downstairs."

"Definitely not," she said without compunction. "At this moment in time I have other priorities." Although her career and business were important, Marc would always come first.

"And what might those priories be?" he asked as he ran his fingers through her hair.

"You...us...here and now, and to love you," she told him, and it was the truth. She meant what she was saying with all her heart.

"Kate, you don't know how much you mean to me and how much I love you," he said passionately as he buried his face in the hollow of her neck. He inhaled deeply. Capturing her. It was as if he was taking her deep inside and making her a part of him.

"Show me," she said, and gently finding his lips with hers, she silenced him with kisses.

His hard, searching lips brushed against hers, and she was open and waiting for him to take her. Once again Marc was in control, and Kate was willingly surrendering to his needs.

She was Marc's. She would always be Marc's. And as he took her to rapturous heights with his lovemaking she knew she was where she wanted to be. She was safe and she was in his arms.

ABOUT THE AUTHOR

Arabella Sheen is a British author of sensual, romantic love stories.

She likes nothing more than the challenge of a blank page, starting a new novel and seeing where the story takes her.

One of the many things Arabella loves to do is to read, and when she's not reading or writing romance, she is either on her allotment sowing and planting with the seasons, or she is sat on the sofa pandering to the demands of her attention-seeking cat.

Having worked and lived in the city of Amsterdam in the Netherlands for nearly twenty years as a theatre nurse, she now lives in the South West of England with her family.

Social Media

Website: www.arabellasheen.co.uk
Twitter: @ArabellaSheen
Facebook: @ArabellaSheenAuthor

www.ingramcontent.com/pod-product-compliance
Lightning Source LLC
Chambersburg PA
CBHW071251170626
46809CB00001B/176